THE TROUBLE WITH ITALIAN MILLIONAIRES

KARIN BAINE

ROMANCE

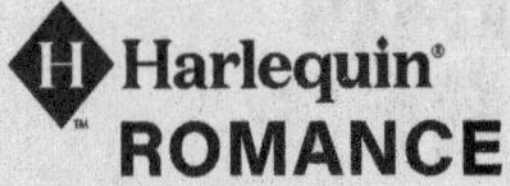

ISBN-13: 978-1-335-47079-9

The Trouble with Italian Millionaires

For questions and comments about the quality of this book, please contact us at CustomerService@Harlequin.com.

Harlequin Enterprises ULC
22 Adelaide St. West, 41st Floor
Toronto, Ontario M5H 4E3, Canada
www.Harlequin.com

HarperCollins Publishers
Macken House, 39/40 Mayor Street Upper,
Dublin 1, D01 C9W8, Ireland
www.HarperCollins.com

Printed in U.S.A.

1 2 3 4 5 6 7 8 9 10 HDC 28 27 26 25

A Pact Between Tycoons

Friends by choice... Brothers by law!

Enzo Capelli and Alexandros Galatis have been partners in crime since university, cultivating wild reputations by throwing parties, wreaking havoc and breaking hearts. The one line they vow never to cross? Dating each other's sister!

Enzo is a man of his word. But when Alex's gorgeous sister, Thaleia, asks for his help with a fake dating scheme, he's willing—after all, it's not real. Yet under moonlit Mediterranean skies, their sizzling chemistry soon threatens to consume them both...

Read Enzo's story in

The Trouble with Italian Millionaires by Karin Baine

When tragedy strikes, Alex finds himself father to a little boy he never knew he had. Wholly unprepared for fatherhood, he's in need of a tutor for his son, and when Enzo's sister, Beatrice, arrives on Ithaca to be interviewed, Alex knows she's the only woman for the job—and his heart!

Read Alex's story in

Falling for the Grumpy Greek by Suzanne Merchant

Both available now!

Dear Reader,

I'm sure we've all thought about running away to a small island to get away from our problems, and that's exactly what Thaleia Galatis does when she's jilted at the altar. What she hasn't realized is that she needs a millionaire on a superyacht to complete her new life. Cue Enzo Capelli sailing in to create his own brand of chaos and completely go against the no-sisters pact he made with her brother, Alexandros, at university.

I hope you enjoy this visit to sun-drenched Greece and the love story that unfolds on the shores.

Karin x

Karin Baine lives in Northern Ireland with her husband, two sons and her out-of-control notebook collection. Her mother and her grandmother's vast collection of books inspired her love of reading and her dream of becoming a Harlequin author. Now she can tell people she has a *proper* job! You can follow Karin on X @karinbaine1 or visit her website for the latest news, karinbaine.com.

Books by Karin Baine

Harlequin Romance

Princesses' Night Out

Temptation in a Tiara

Pregnant Princess at the Altar
Highland Fling with Her Boss
Cinderella's Festive Fake Date
The Tycoon's Festive Houseguest

Harlequin Medical Romance

Christmas North and South

Festive Fling with the Surgeon

Jet Set Docs

Spanish Doc to Heal Her

Royal Docs

Surgeon Prince's Fake Fiancée
A Mother for His Little Princess

Nurse's New Year with the Billionaire
Tempted by Her Off-Limits Boss
A Nurse, a Pup, a Second Chance

Visit the Author Profile page
at Harlequin.com for more titles.

With thanks to Elena, Jenny and Suzanne
for their patience x

CHAPTER ONE

THE COOL ISLAND breeze was a welcome reprieve from the intense heat. Thaleia often left the blue doors and shutters on her white-washed shop open so it wouldn't get too stifling for her customers. Mostly tourists, though she did get some custom jewellery orders from Greece's most prominent figures, likely through her mother's referral, she suspected.

Thaleia didn't need to work for a living. Not when she was the daughter of Nicholas and Helena Galatis. She could have lived off the family name and wealth for the rest of her life, but she'd needed more.

Being jilted at the altar had a way of making her reassess her life. Since then, the privileged life she'd led in the spotlight, making her fodder for the gossip columns, no longer appealed to her.

She'd struggled to find a purpose, and had signed up for jewellery-making classes as a way of simply getting out of the house, and distracting her from her thoughts.

Thaleia had grown up thinking she would marry the love of her life—from the right family, of course—and raise children of her own. Only to have that dream taken away from her. She hadn't wanted a loveless relationship like her parents, whose marriage had seemed more of a power move than a love match. More concerned with status and appearance than one another, it seemed, by the number of rows that had gone on at home.

After having her heart broken by Makis, and her dreams smashed, Thaleia had realised she couldn't pin all her hopes on a man as her parents had intended. She had to have a life of her own.

So she'd learned how to make her own jewellery and moved to this island. Paxos was the smallest island group of Ionian islands, south of Corfu. Far enough away from her parents in Athens, and the island of Ithaca, where their family had ruled in ancient times, for her to create a whole new life for herself. The shop wasn't some high-end establishment in a city, but a converted villa by the sea. Big enough to house her living quarters and a small workshop where she sold her creations to passing tourists. She loved her new, quiet existence, knowing it was hers and no one could take it away from her. As long as she made a success of it.

It was early days but she was enjoying her independence. Waking up in the sunshine, eating her breakfast on the patio in the shade provided by the surrounding olive trees, then starting work on her own premises, she was the most at peace she'd felt in a long time.

'Good morning, Thaleia. Is there anything you'd like today?' Her elderly neighbour, Agathi, appeared at the open door as she always did at this time of the morning.

She was pulling a small cart of delicious home-made pastries and pies, which she sold around the island.

'Morning. Can I have some *spanakopita*, please?' Thaleia set down the file she'd been using to smooth down the edges on the dragonfly pendant that she'd cut from a flat piece of silver.

'Of course.' Agathi put a spinach pie into the brown paper bag and slipped in some *loukoumades* too before handing it over.

Thaleia raised an eyebrow at the fried dough balls topped with sugar and cinnamon, which she hadn't asked for.

'You need fattening up, Miss Thaleia. You're too skinny. Men like a little meat on the bone.' Although the woman's words could have been construed as insulting, and not very PC these days, it was hard to take offence when she meant well.

Since Thaleia had arrived, the old woman had regularly checked in on her, and, with no apparent family of her own, seemed to have adopted Thaleia. It was nice to have someone looking out for her while at the same time letting her have her independence. A novelty for someone who'd lived her life so far according to what her parents had wanted for her.

Thaleia smiled. Not bothering to argue that she wasn't looking for another man. Heartbreak might have been good for her figure, but it had also brought some trust issues that would likely stop her from giving her heart away too easily again in the future.

Paid, and with other customers to see before the sun rose too high in the sky, the woman set off with her wares. Leaving Thaleia alone again.

She put her glasses on and concentrated on soldering the setting in the main body of the insect she'd been working on. This piece would have to be cleaned and polished in the special solution to make the silver shine before she added any stones. As it was simply a project for herself, she'd selected a semi-precious aquamarine for the centre.

She'd stocked the shop with her other creations—

brooches and pendants—all with a nod to the beautiful sea that surrounded her.

Her signature blue and green tones were to be found in the decorative enamel and precious stones she worked with. All a labour of love, but this little dragonfly was special. It represented a new beginning for her, and she hoped by making her business a success she could put the past behind her.

She was tumbling the little pendant along with some of her other recent makes in the special solution, her back to the door, when she heard the shop bell ring again.

'Thanks, Agathi, but I don't really want any more pastries. I'll get fat and then no man will want me.'

This was usually the part where her elderly neighbour tutted and said something about her needing a husband and babies, before leaving another pastry on the counter. Except the only reply was an awkward cough that sounded decidedly unlike Agathi.

Thaleia spun around to come face to face with a very tall, very handsome man staring at her in amusement. His grin showing off a lovely pair of dimples as well as a mouthful of even white teeth.

Immediately feeling self-conscious, she snatched her safety glasses off and wiped her hands on a towel. It wasn't the most glamorous job behind the scenes. When she was working, she tied her hair up into a high bun and donned old clothes under her tatty apron. She was already regretting the stained white vest-top and garish peacock-feather-patterned yoga pants.

'For the record, I think you're perfect as you are, and you will never have a problem catching a man's attention.' Smooth. Very smooth. And very Italian. The sort of man she might have fallen for in the past, but these days she was much more cynical and less likely to let the flattery from a stranger go to her head. Even if her face was burning at the compliment.

'Sorry. I thought you were someone else. How can I help you?' She decided it was best not to swoon, or roll her eyes, and simply disregard his cheesy comment. Goodness knew she needed as many compliments as she could get.

Perhaps realising that his sweet-talking wasn't going to get him anywhere with her, he switched off flirty mode and got down to business.

'I'm looking to commission something for a very special lady,' he said, holding her gaze. His eyes were a curious grey-green. Along with his slicked-back black hair and natural tan, he cut a dashing figure.

Thaleia grabbed her pad of paper and a pencil. 'Do you have anything in mind?' She was curious if it was an engagement ring he wanted when he seemed like the kind of man who left broken hearts everywhere he went rather than settle down. Not least because he was flirting with her. A stranger.

He was probably a passenger on one of the cruise ships that stopped frequently in the main port of Gaios so rich tourists could come and spend their money on local souvenirs. Something she wouldn't dare sneer at when it was their trade that was keeping her afloat at the minute. This man before her certainly had money. She could tell by the expensive watch and the way he dressed. Although he was in casual attire—cargo shorts, loafers and a coral polo shirt—she knew it was all designer gear. She'd been around enough rich boys to recognise it.

'I want a necklace. Something tasteful.'

'A pendant, or something more substantial?' The difference would be in the price as well as the time and effort it would take for her to make something elaborate.

'It's for Irida Angelopoulos. I'm sure you've heard of her. She's a good friend of mine and I want to give her something special for her birthday. Perhaps I should leave the decisions entirely up to you.' The casual way he said it would sound to anyone as though he were ordering a pizza. When Thaleia was aware his 'special friend' was one of Greece's most famous socialites.

It was a daunting prospect, but she also knew the exposure this would give her might just be the boost her business needed.

'You would trust me to do that?'

'Sure. I've seen your work online.'

Thaleia eyed him warily. There was something familiar about him, but she couldn't put her finger on it. 'How did you hear about my business?'

He dismissed any suspicion with a wave of his hand. 'I saw something in the papers a while ago. When Irida invited me to her celebrations on the island in a week's time, I thought I'd call in and see if you could help me with the perfect gift for her.'

'It doesn't give me much notice. I'd have to work solely on this piece.' It would be a huge undertaking, not only in terms of her workload, but responsibility too.

Another dismissive wave. 'I'm prepared to pay whatever it costs to get you to create something special for the occasion.'

'Oh. I will need to take a sizeable deposit to secure the job.' She didn't want to waste her time designing something only to discover he'd sailed off into the sunset.

The man produced a leather wallet from his pocket and slid out a credit card.

'And how will I be able to contact you, Mr… Capelli, to discuss my progress?' She checked the name on the card, and it rang a bell somewhere in the back of her brain.

He slid her pad and pencil over to his side of the counter and jotted down his information. 'That's my number. Call any time. I'm anchored out there in my yacht, *Bacchus*.'

Of course he was.

*Bacchus… Bacchus…*that sounded familiar too. Then it hit her. Bacchus and Dionysus. The nicknames her older brother, Alexandros, and his friend Enzo had given themselves when they'd studied together at Cambridge University in England.

'Enzo,' she said, the penny finally dropping. Although they'd never met, she knew him by reputation and some old photographs she'd seen of Alex's uni days.

If she'd thought her brother had gone off the rails for a while when he'd moved abroad, the tales he'd told of Enzo's antics had been even more shocking.

She blamed the man in front of her entirely for corrupting her brother.

'The one and only.' The grin was back in

place, only less disarming now that she was aware of who she was dealing with.

'So, you didn't simply happen by my shop.' Thaleia narrowed her eyes at him and folded her arms, wondering what game he was playing with her. As far as she knew, Alex was more concerned with being a father than still partying with Enzo, so why he was here toying with her was a mystery.

Although it had taken the tragedy of little Georgios's mother dying in a car accident for Alex to find out he'd fathered a child he hadn't known existed, it had been the making of him.

He'd given up the hedonistic lifestyle Enzo was presumably still living, and settled down into fatherhood, finally becoming a mature, responsible adult. The last thing her brother needed was this man-child upending everything and disrupting the stable childhood he was trying to establish for his son.

'Well, I did. Sort of. I just happened to know that you're also Dionysus's little sister.'

Thaleia rolled her eyes. Naming each other after the gods of wine and chaos was everything she needed to know about the two men who'd been almost like brothers back in the day, according to Alex.

She would admit to having felt a little jealous at the time. Left out of all the fun, back home, still under the command of her controlling father, though she understood why that little bit of freedom had gone to Alex's head. He and her father had clashed a lot. Whereas, until recently, she'd simply done as she was bid. Not wanting to cause any more tension at home.

It hadn't been an easy upbringing despite the wealth and privilege they were constantly reminded that their father had provided for them. A stifling environment, which wasn't helped by her parents' odd relationship. Where most children were the product of love between husband and wife, she and Alex had been the product of a marriage that seemed to be more of a business arrangement. She'd never witnessed any genuine affection between them. It hadn't made for a particularly loving environment. Perhaps that was why she'd gone searching for it in the wrong place.

She'd been convinced that Makis would provide her with that sense of love and romance she'd never really experienced. Too swept away by the fantasy to realise he was having cold feet about committing to one woman for the rest of his life. And he'd been too cowardly to tell her so. Instead, he'd publicly humiliated her by failing to turn up on their wedding day. Leaving her at the altar alone in front of Greece's most prominent families and figures. She'd thought she'd never be able to show her face again. Not that she'd wanted to leave the house at all, broken-hearted and wondering what she'd done wrong to make him not want to be with her any more.

It had been some time later she'd discovered he'd been partying in Ibiza, making up for lost time with every other woman taken in by his charm and good looks without a thought for what he'd put her through.

He and Enzo would have got on well. One more reason to take a dislike to the man standing in front of her. Not only responsible for corrupting her brother, but he reminded her too much of her Peter Pan ex who didn't want to grow up.

'So, what is it that you actually want, Enzo?' Thaleia sighed, handing back his credit card, her big commission and dreams slipping away from her. He was just another spoiled rich boy having fun at her expense. This was likely some prank that he would regale his pals with later.

'I told you. A gift for my friend.'

Thaleia tutted her displeasure. 'Why me? I'm sure there are a hundred other, more established jewellers who'd be falling over themselves for your business.'

He raised a dark eyebrow. 'And you don't want it?'

He had her there. It wasn't every day an opportunity like this came along. If it was genuine. The business couldn't survive selling tourist trinkets alone. Key rings and earrings weren't going to pay the bills, and she wanted to prove to herself, and everyone, that she wasn't a failure. That she was more than a weeping bride standing alone at the altar.

'I want to know why you chose me.'

Enzo shrugged. 'I did read about you in the papers, and I was in the vicinity, as I said. I was curious to meet you after years of Alex talking about his little sister.'

'Did Alex send you to check up on me?' She knew her family didn't believe she could make this work. It would be just like her big brother to send someone to spy on her and offer the chance of work out of pity. But she didn't want charity or to live off the family name. She needed something that was just hers.

'I've hardly heard from Alex since he became boring.'

Thaleia frowned. She knew her brother had changed, but, in her opinion, it was for the better. 'You mean since he became a mature, responsible adult? I think it was about time one of you did.'

Enzo clutched his chest, though the grin remained in place. 'Ouch.'

'He's a good father to Georgios and not interested in drinking or parties any more.'

'Like I said, boring.'

'Look, if you've just come here to insult my brother—'

'I didn't. I miss him. I guess I was curious about you since I'm here, but I honestly need this gift.'

Thaleia's mind was working overtime. The last thing she needed in her life was a handsome, smooth-talking party boy, but a high-profile commission was something she simply couldn't afford to turn down.

With a sigh and a roll of her eyes she finally said, 'Fine. I'll see what I can do.'

After all, it wasn't as though he were going to be in her life for too long. She mightn't have to see him again until the piece was finished.

Despite his good looks, Enzo was not the sort of man she should get involved with and as long as she remembered that, there shouldn't be a problem.

Enzo hadn't been able to resist calling in on Alex's little sister. He'd heard enough about her over the years to imagine he knew her. Though meeting her in person had exceeded all expectations.

It was no wonder his best friend had insisted on the 'no sisters' pact even though their paths hadn't crossed until now. They'd sowed their wild oats in their university days, but when they'd discovered they both had younger sisters, they'd wanted to protect them from the life they led. If their paths were ever to cross in the future, they'd agreed that both sisters were off limits. Not wanting either of their siblings to be left upset the way countless partners had been when they'd moved on to the next pretty girl who took their eye. Even though the likelihood of that had seemed minuscule at the time.

Thaleia was stunning. Her dark hair caught up in a messy top knot showed off her delicate features. Olive-green eyes framed by dark lashes and brows, a perfect nose and full lips, she was beautiful even dressed in what he supposed was her work garb. It was little wonder Alex had never let them meet.

When Enzo had received his invitation to Irida's party, he'd remembered reading about Thaleia's new business venture on the same island. She'd been featured more in the papers ever since she'd been jilted at the altar. That had been a big news story and he'd felt for her at the time, her life and character picked apart for the gossip columns. Not that he'd heard any of the news from Alex himself. Their relationship seemed to have tapered off these last couple of years, dwindling down to the odd phone call or text. Ever since Alex had discovered he'd fathered a baby during the latter days of Bacchus and Dionysus's hedonistic ways, he'd changed. Their way of life, and Enzo himself, apparently not what he wanted any more.

He understood that Alex had different priorities now, but that didn't mean he wasn't a little hurt at being pushed aside. Perhaps he wasn't the perfect role model for Alex's new addition, but it wasn't as though he'd take the boy clubbing. He was sure Alex could still do with a listening ear every now and then, the way he could. Catching up over the phone wasn't the same as seeing each other or being involved in one another's lives. Alex was the brother Enzo never had and he wanted that connection back.

Perhaps, subconsciously, coming here had been Enzo's way of trying to reconnect with him in some way. Even though they lived very different lives these days.

He missed his old friend and the antics they used to get up to. Drinks and women had been their staple diet, living life exactly how they wanted to. Not answerable to anyone. In Alex's case, university had been his escape from his father's control. In Enzo's case, a respite away from the trauma of losing his parents in a cable-car accident when he was eighteen. The care of his eight-year-old sister, Beatrice, had been left to him, and though he'd done his best to help her, he'd worried he wasn't enough. It had been too much for a grieving son and brother to ever cope with on his own. So he'd sent Beatrice to a boarding school in England, convinced the staff there could look after her better than he ever could. Although he'd visited often, and he'd gone to Cambridge University so they were still close. The rest was history. He'd been living his life the same way since, and happy doing so.

Though Alex becoming a father had changed everything between them. With Georgios being Alex's main priority, and Enzo suddenly on the outside looking in, it felt like being abandoned all over again. Alex had always been his anchor. There when Enzo had needed him. Without him, Enzo had been adrift. So he'd carried on with what he was used to. Partying. It was easy to make friends when he had money and his own yacht. Though nothing had ever come close to the bond he'd had with Alex. Everyone else seemed like a poor substitute in comparison.

Given Thaleia's change in attitude since realising who he was, it was clear Alex had shared tales of Dionysus's and Bacchus's misadventures. No wonder she'd been looking at him with undisguised disdain. Enzo knew his past misdeeds wouldn't shower him in glory but he wouldn't apologise. It was who he was. At least since his parents had died. A reminder that life had to be lived to the fullest and he had been making the most of it every day since.

In terms of financial status, he was lucky. It was his parents' premature and tragic deaths that enabled him to lead this nomadic life, having inherited their shipping business and estate. With people running everything on his behalf, it meant he didn't have to put down roots, and he was free to go wherever he chose, whenever he pleased. Like today, sailing to Paxos to order bespoke jewellery for his friend's party.

In his mind he'd imagined a pampered princess here playing shop, her minions doing the actual work. It hadn't occurred to him that she'd be getting her own hands dirty making the jewellery herself. Working for a living. Already making her a better person than he was.

'You're more than welcome to come on board the yacht to discuss details.' He couldn't resist riling her again. Knowing she couldn't wait to get shot of him. It wasn't often that women resisted his charms and he found it a novelty. A challenge. Thaleia Galatis was out of bounds for a multitude of reasons, including his and Alex's pact never to go near one another's sisters. Yet, Enzo was inextricably drawn to her. Akin to a child pulling the pigtails of the girl he liked, he wanted to get her attention. Propositioning her seemed the easiest way to do it.

'I don't think that would be a very good idea.' Her lips were pursed in blatant disapproval. Which only spurred him on, as he knew she wouldn't think twice about putting him in his place. Something that didn't happen very often to him.

'Some dinner…a little wine…' He waggled his eyebrows suggestively, having way too much fun watching her temperature rise. The only reason he felt comfortable flirting with Alex's little sister was because he knew she wasn't interested and there was no chance of her reciprocating. He admired the fact that she didn't feel the need to impress him or appease him. She was more than capable of speaking her mind.

'It doesn't sound much like a business meeting to me.' She squinted her eyes at him, sussing out his motives immediately and proving his point.

'There's nothing to say that business has to be boring. Besides, the yacht is my office as well as my home. I conduct all of my affairs on board. Sometimes even in the hot tub.' His deliberately provocative comment provoked the reaction he'd anticipated as she rolled her eyes and tutted at him.

'Well, that's not how I do business. I'll sketch a few ideas and get them to you tomorrow. Once I get your approval on a design, there will be no reason to see one another until it's completed.'

'Whatever you say, Ms Galatis. You're the boss.' Without thinking, he reached out and took her hand, kissing it before taking his leave. Keeping his eye on her as he did so. Watching her sour expression change to shock and back.

Her flushed cheeks showed he'd made an impact, even if it was sheer annoyance.

'Thank you, Mr Capelli. Now, if you don't mind, I've got a lot of work to do.' That was her way of dismissing him once and for all and Enzo made his exit.

He didn't want to make her uncomfortable, just wanted to get to know her a little better.

CHAPTER TWO

THALEIA YAWNED. HER MIND had been working overtime last night, refusing to quiet and let her get a good night's sleep. Her thoughts and dreams had revolved around, not only potential jewellery designs, but also Enzo Capelli.

Somehow she'd imagined years of debauchery would have caught up with him by now. The indulgent lifestyle he apparently led meant that he should have a bulging waistline and a ruddy complexion at the least. Not so. He'd obviously been taking care of himself in some fashion. She only had a vague recollection of what the infamous 'Bacchus' had looked like in his university days, but he was still a stunning-looking man now.

The striking grey-green eyes against tanned skin and dark hair weren't easily forgotten. Even if his playboy reputation immediately rang alarm bells for her.

Thaleia didn't know if she'd ever trust another man after Makis had betrayed her so selfishly.

What she was certain of was that she couldn't afford to be swayed by good looks when Enzo was evidently a man who would never dream of settling down when he had the world at his feet.

In an effort to try and regain control of the situation, she'd texted the number he'd given her and arranged an appointment at the shop at midday. Somewhere she felt comfortable and in charge, that would emphasise that she was only interested in business, nothing else.

As she rearranged the sketches of her designs on the counter, her stomach tied itself in knots. It meant a lot to her to get this right when it had the potential to put her on the map.

She watched the hands on the clock above her workbench meet at twelve and keep ticking. The later he was for this appointment, the more irritated she became. Time was money when she was self-employed. No longer enjoying the lazy mornings and the devil-may-care approach Enzo no doubt took when it came to the working day.

When the shop bell rang, however, it wasn't a tall Italian charmer who walked in, but a squat, bulldog-like figure who stalked up to the counter.

'Ms Galatis?'

She nodded, wondering what he wanted with her. He certainly didn't look like a man who'd go jewellery shopping. At least not without a balaclava and a shotgun.

Thaleia swallowed hard. 'How can I help you?'

'Mr Capelli sends his apologies. He can't make it ashore today.'

Thaleia frowned. She should have known he was just going to mess her around. Especially since she'd made it clear she wasn't interested in anything other than a business relationship. He was probably hungover, lying in bed with some buxom blonde, and had decided he couldn't be bothered to follow up with her after yesterday.

She could have kicked herself for forgetting to take that deposit from him when she'd obviously wasted precious time and energy on what she'd thought was an important commission. The next time she spoke with Alex she'd make sure to let him know what she thought of his 'friend'. Though, given their already strained relationship, she doubted it would make any difference.

She began gathering her sketches, ready to dump them in the bin.

'Mr Capelli asks if you'd care to join him on board his yacht for a spot of lunch so you can talk…business.'

A classic power move. Thaleia was already regretting getting involved with the man in any capacity when he was proving to be so frustrating. Her first reaction was to say, 'Absolutely not,' and leave things there. However, they both knew this was a big deal for her. Enzo held all the cards and he was playing his hand. It was down to her whether to fold or go all in.

If these last months had taught her anything it was that she was tougher than she gave herself credit for. She wasn't going to lose out on the opportunity of a lifetime just to save face. Just this once she'd let him play the upper hand. Next time they'd do things on her terms.

'When?' she asked, wondering if she had time to change.

'Now. The yacht tender is waiting to take you.' He was making it hard for her to say no.

Although Thaleia had mixed with the wealthy and privileged her entire life, been on more yachts than she could count, it didn't mean she wasn't curious about getting a peek into Enzo Capelli's world. To see if 'Bacchus' was still alive and well.

'Just give me a minute to get my things together.'

The man gave her a nod and stepped outside the shop. She heard the strike of a match, which was followed by the smell of cigarette smoke. A horrible habit, but something that was giving her a moment of privacy to check her reflection before leaving. She didn't wish to appear dishevelled, as though Enzo had ruffled her feathers with this little trick.

She had dressed for a business meeting in a plain white blouse and a navy pencil skirt and she wasn't about to change now. The location might have changed, but her mindset hadn't. No matter what Enzo Capelli might have planned, this was purely a business decision. With that in mind, she didn't bother retouching her make-up. She was out to impress him, not with her looks, but with her work.

The spray on her face as they sped the short distance to the yacht in the small tender boat was refreshing. Since moving here she'd barely had time to enjoy the beautiful surroundings. Busy with setting up the shop and stocking it with inventory. She supposed she took it all for granted. A side effect of growing up wanting for nothing, never appreciating what she did have. It wasn't until she'd felt as though she'd lost it all that she'd begun to see things differently. The struggle to come back from being jilted at the altar had been difficult, but with time she'd begun to get back to her old self. Only with a tougher skin. The experience had made her wary of trusting anyone, becoming too reliant on someone else to make her happy. Now she was doing all she could to make that happen herself, and, so far, things were going well. Thaleia didn't want anything, or anyone, to spoil the life she was building for herself.

This was simply a moment to sit back and enjoy the sun. Eyes closed, head tilted back, she felt the heat from the rays like a warm hug. Something she'd been missing for a long time.

'Sleeping on the job?' There was no mistaking that silky Italian voice.

When Thaleia opened her eyes it was to see Enzo staring down at her from the yacht, a smile spread across his face. She hated that he'd interrupted her moment of peace, but the sooner this was over, the better.

'Well, I was awake all night working for you, Mr Capelli. I told you my time is precious. That's why I don't appreciate any disruption to my schedule. I had to close my shop to make this trip out here when it was something we could have wrapped up during our appointment.' She said the last word deliberately so he would realise that it was he who'd broken their contract, inconveniencing her when he likely had all day to lounge about.

'Sorry about that.' He held out his hand and helped her on board. 'I had some last-minute calls to make and I thought it would be nice for you to take a break.'

'That should have been my decision to make.'

As she stepped onto the deck, she stumbled and had to steady herself against him. Aware of his smooth, muscular chest beneath her fingers. His white cotton shirt providing no barrier between them since he'd left it open, billowing in the breeze.

Such simple, brief contact shouldn't have made her heart race and her mouth go dry, but she supposed it was the first time she'd even touched a man since her non-wedding. She was bound to be a little nervy.

'Yes. Sorry. But I just thought you were taking the time to see me anyway…' He seemed as likely to argue the point as she was and Thaleia didn't want to prolong her time here any longer than necessary so she bit her tongue. He'd get the idea soon enough that she wasn't going to be easily impressed with his money or status, and would be speeding back to her own territory very soon.

'I just wanted to finalise the design with you before I get started.' She pulled her sketches from the bag she'd slung over her shoulder at the last minute before leaving the shop.

'Of course. After we've had some lunch. That sea air will have made you hungry, as well as thirsty.' He stepped aside and gestured at the table, which had already been laid for two. Her participation in his little scheme apparently a foregone conclusion. It irked her, of course it did, but she held her tongue. For now.

They moved to the small table and he pulled out a chair for her. At least he possessed some manners, it seemed.

Attentive waiters brought plates of stuffed cucumber bites, filled with feta, olives and tomatoes. Followed by chicken souvlaki skewers with tzatziki and grilled vegetables. Too tempting to resist. She didn't stop for lunch usually, powering through, courtesy of her next-door neighbour's produce, which she ate as she worked. Though Thaleia wouldn't admit it, it was nice to have time out and have someone fuss around her for a little while. As long as she didn't fall into old habits and get used to it. Becoming complacent had caused all her troubles so far.

She'd taken it for granted that she'd get married and have a family, live happily ever after. When that had been taken from her, she'd been left with nothing. It had taken her this long to build herself back up—she wasn't going to take the chance of losing herself again. As long as she kept in mind this whole scene by Enzo was likely a façade. A window dressing to disguise whatever it was he really wanted from her.

'You really shouldn't have gone to so much trouble, Mr Capelli.'

'Enzo, please.' Enzo clattered his cutlery down on the now empty plate in front of him.

'Enzo. I really did come here just to show you my designs.'

He huffed out a breath and waved the waiters over to clear the table. 'If you must.'

Thaleia held her temper in check as she tried once again to get him to focus on her sketches. 'Now, I did a little bit of research on your "friend". Irida does seem to favour blue. A lot of her fashion choices are in shades of azure. That's why I thought perhaps something with sapphires and diamonds? According to your budget and preference, of course.'

She'd agonised over the designs, wanting the piece to be something meaningful and personal. Which meant trying to get to know this famous woman through all the stories and photographs that had been taken of her over the years. Irida, although in her sixties, perhaps older, seemed to be something of a party girl herself, renowned for her days-long soirées and long line of toyboy exes. A wealthy socialite who appeared to enjoy the limelight. Though Thaleia knew from personal experience whatever was in the public domain wasn't always necessarily a true depiction.

She'd had to endure countless false tales about why her wedding had been called off at the last minute. Most of which had lain the blame entirely at her feet. According to 'sources' and 'friends' of her ex, she'd pushed Makis into the marriage, or it had been a power move between the families that he'd decided not to be a part of in the end. All false, but no one wanted to hear the boring truth that the man was too cowardly to commit. Not that she'd wanted to share that humiliation with the world anyway.

Here, away from the family home, she'd hoped to escape all thoughts of that time. Although she couldn't forget it altogether, it was projects like this one that would hopefully keep her distracted, at least.

'I believe she has a beautiful garden and I thought perhaps a simple design in the shape of a flower would make a nice pendant and earrings set. A single sapphire surrounded by teardrop diamonds. I can also make the same pieces with semi-precious stones if you'd prefer?' She looked up for the first time to find him staring at her rather than the designs. The intensity of his gaze making her insides flutter like the yacht sails in the breeze.

He smiled. 'No, sapphires and diamonds sound perfect.'

'Good. I had another idea. It's a bit…out there, I suppose, but I thought I'd get a little creative and see what you think.' She pointed to the sketch she'd slaved over most. Her creative vision of something she hoped was as personal to his friend as it was to her.

The pendant was made up of several strands of sapphires curved into a wave, crested with small diamonds. Representing the beautiful blue water that surrounded the island. The design was special to her, something she was proud of, and she hoped Enzo would like it too so she would get to bring it to life.

'This is the one.' This time he showed interest, picking up the sheet of paper to study the design closer. Thaleia could barely wipe the smile off her face.

'I can set it in silver or white gold. Suspend it on a simple chain or repeat the design the whole way around the necklace...whatever you think.' Although that version was more expensive, and perhaps would make more of an impact, she preferred the simplicity of her original design.

However, the choice was Enzo's. He was the customer, after all.

'White gold, and I think the pendant shows off the design best, don't you?' The way he was still studying it made her believe he was being honest and not simply telling her what he thought she wanted to hear.

'Yes. I, er, think so too.' Thaleia did her best to ignore the smidgeon of admiration creeping in towards him. Even if he had provided her with a lovely lunch in beautiful surroundings, he had dragged her all the way out here when they could just as easily have finalised this at the shop.

'That's settled, then.' Enzo picked up the bottle of wine and began to top up their glasses.

Thaleia covered hers with her hand. 'No more for me, thanks. I need to keep a clear head while I'm working. Speaking of which, I should really get back to the shop.'

'What's the hurry? You should really learn to slow down, Thaleia, and enjoy life.'

It was easy for him to say that when he clearly didn't have any commitments or responsibilities. She'd heard enough from Alex to understand the kind of life Enzo led out here at sea. Ruler of all he surveyed. But that didn't include her. She lived in the real world, which she was keen to get back to, away from the handsome Italian who seemed determined to make her spend time with him.

She was wary of doing so because she was attracted to him, despite all the red flags. She was still nursing the wounds from her failed relationship and Enzo Capelli wasn't the sort of man she should show any weakness to. He was definitely the 'love them and leave them' type, and getting involved with someone like that was only asking for more heartbreak. Regardless of the past, she still yearned for a husband and children, and anything less was selling herself short. Something she was determined not to do.

Thaleia knew she had a lot of love to give, but she also needed it returned. Growing up in a house so lacking in it had only made her crave a family of her own. To finally fill that void in her life that her parents' relationship had left inside her. Knowing there was more to marriage and a home than money and status, and wanting to experience it, live it, herself.

'I'm enjoying my life here, thank you very much. The reason I have a busy work schedule is because you want a rush on a very special commission. Something I'm happy to do, but that means working, not lunching with you. So, if you don't mind, I'd appreciate it if you could arrange my return to the island.' Thaleia packed her things away, ready to leave as soon as possible now that she'd achieved what she'd come out here to do.

'That could take a while,' Enzo said, swilling the wine in his glass before draining it.

Thaleia felt all the blood drain from her body. 'Why?'

'It's going to take us a while to turn around again.' Enzo gestured around.

Only then did Thaleia realise that they'd left the island. The vista of trees and villas had disappeared. Now there was only sea as far as the eye could see. Even though it was futile, she found herself running towards the railings to look over the side. Half of her wondering if she could swim back. Suddenly being stuck here with Italy's premier playboy felt a little bit sinister.

'What have you done?' The island was a speck in the distance and she was powerless to do anything about her current situation. Entirely at Enzo's mercy.

He held his hands up, still grinning, as though he'd had nothing to do with what had happened. 'We're just taking a little trip around the island. A change of scenery. We'll be back soon enough.'

The blood returned quickly to her face, along with a burning sense of anger. 'You had no right. I didn't agree to this.'

'No, but I thought it would do you good to have some time out. You appeared to be flat out working yesterday. Nothing like the carefree girl your brother used to talk about. I was hoping to provide you with a little respite. I'll pay whatever overtime you think is necessary.' The man's casual attitude to her work was infuriating to say the least. Obviously, this was a man used to getting what he wanted. People danced to his tune whenever he chose. Except Thaleia had been around those kinds of people her entire life and none of it impressed her. Now it only irritated her. She'd had enough of selfish, thoughtless people.

'That's not the point. You can't just throw money around and expect it to solve everything. I didn't want to come all the way out here. I didn't want to have lunch with you, and I certainly didn't want to go sailing. Which you would have found out if you'd bothered to ask.' Yes, she'd changed from the romantic dreamer who'd thought a husband and family were all that she needed in life. However, being jilted publicly had made her cynical.

At this point she was ready to tell Enzo what he could do with his special commission, only she was effectively being held hostage on board his yacht.

He set his glass down and seemed deep in thought. Eventually he stood up. This time the grin was gone. 'I'm sorry. I suppose I acted rashly. I promise you it was with the best of intentions. I know you don't have a very high opinion of me, likely due to whatever stories you've heard from your brother about our time at university. I simply wanted us to get to know one another a little better. I guess I went about it the wrong way. We'll get you home as soon as possible, and I will recompense you for your time. It's not every day someone turns down an invitation to the yacht and I wanted you to see what you were missing.'

'So you thought kidnapping me was the way to win me over? I don't know what my brother told you about me, but I can assure you I'm not easily won over by an arrogant, showboating playboy. You were right about one thing though—you do know nothing about me, Mr Capelli.' And she intended to keep things that way.

Enzo should have been embarrassed, thoroughly chastised by the Greek beauty before him. Instead, he was in awe of her. Someone who wasn't afraid to put him in his place despite only having met him yesterday, and whom he was paying to work for him. Clearly Thaleia's principles meant more to her than any display of wealth.

He supposed that was mainly because she was used to it, coming from such a wealthy family herself. But there was more to it than that. Her fiery personality told him that this was a woman to be reckoned with, and he liked being around her. It grew tiring at times when the only people around were paid to be there, or were there for what they could get out of him.

That was what had drawn him towards Alex at uni. He didn't stand for any of Enzo's attempts to boss him about. They were equals, and Enzo realised he'd met his match in Thaleia too. Perhaps that was why he found himself wanting to get to know her better. To get to know the woman behind the pursed lips and folded arms, and hopefully prove to her that he wasn't the awful person she assumed he was. OK, so he'd had his moments, but he'd genuinely been trying to do something nice for her. It had backfired in the worst way. Exactly why he needed to know her better, so he could stop messing things up. Even if she was even more beautiful with her temper in full flow. Something he hadn't been aware of since her brother had always described her as easy-going. Enzo supposed people changed. His increasingly distant relationship with Alex was proof of that.

He gave her a minute to calm down and went to inform the captain to take them back. On his return, he found her holding onto the rails, head tilted back, and the wind blowing her dark tresses. She'd worn her hair down today, he'd noted, and, despite the business attire she'd donned, she did actually look more relaxed. Carefree.

'Before you bite my head off again, or accuse me of kidnapping you, I've told the captain to take us back.'

'Thank you.' Her gratitude was still laced with stern disapproval.

'It will take a while to get us turned around. We should make the most of our time here.'

Thaleia rolled her eyes at him. She was obviously determined to think the worst of him.

Enzo sighed. 'I meant you could see around the yacht, or take a soak in the hot tub.'

'I don't have a swimsuit.'

'I'm sure there's something on board from past guests you can use.'

Another roll of the eyes. 'I don't think so.'

'You know, your eyes are going to roll right out of your head if you keep doing that. I'm doing my best here to make things up to you. I promise I'm not some sort of sleaze who lured you here under false pretences so I can have my wicked way with you.'

'Really?' She arched a disbelieving eyebrow at him.

That might have been part of his repertoire a while ago, but he had been trying, and failing, to make a better second impression on her. She was Alex's little sister, and there was no way he wanted to upset either of them. He didn't want to give Alex any more reason to keep his distance, so attempting to seduce his off-limits sibling certainly wasn't going to endear Enzo to his once best friend. If anything, he wanted her to give a good report back, and hopefully one day he and Alex might be able to resurrect the relationship they once had.

'Really. Believe it or not, I'm just trying to be nice. Maybe I'm out of practice.' Although it was meant as a joke, and it did raise a laugh from his reluctant companion, there was some truth in what he said. He never usually had to try to make someone like him, and took it for granted that everyone loved him. At least, that was what everyone told him when they were guzzling champagne in his hot tub.

What was it she called him? Arrogant. Oh, yes, and she'd accused him of showboating. Guilty as charged. It was how he made friends. A playboy? That too, he supposed. Yeah, Thaleia had nailed him on sight, and the reason he didn't like it was because it was all true. She'd held a mirror up to the man he'd become, and for the first time Enzo wasn't appreciating the view.

Since his parents had died, he hadn't had to try hard at anything. Everything was there for him on a plate. Except a healthy relationship with his little sister. Guilt that he'd failed her had kept him from staying in regular contact. They led separate lives, and instead of being close to the only family he had, they were miles apart. Emotionally, and physically.

It meant he was lonely. He had no one. While that was good for someone who didn't want any ties, there were times he wished he had loved ones around him. Like Christmas, or birthdays. Occasions when he made sure the yacht was always full to capacity with revellers. That was probably why he partied so hard even now. Being the one people gravitated towards for a good time. Because it masked the loneliness for a time. Although, once everyone had gone back to their real lives, he was often left with that terrible void in his chest.

His own fault, of course, for distancing himself from Beatrice, and he wished he could find some way of fixing things between them. However, he couldn't convince himself he deserved her forgiveness, even if she could find a way to give it to him. She'd been a grieving child, and though he'd thought boarding school would give her the structure he couldn't provide, in hindsight he wasn't so sure. He hadn't been there for her emotionally, and he was learning how lonely that place was when he didn't have Alex or Beatrice in his everyday life.

The yacht was his safe place. Living this seemingly carefree life meant he didn't have to deal with his emotions. He'd come to learn that love and family meant only pain for him.

Travelling to a new place, meeting new people, having more parties, and filling his life with enough frivolity he hoped he wouldn't notice it lacked any real meaning.

Thaleia sighed. 'OK. Perhaps I have been a bit spiky. After everything I've heard about you it's possible I judged you a little harshly. I suppose if my brother likes you, you can't be all bad.'

She was still studying him with suspicious, big green eyes, and Enzo knew he was going to have to be on his best behaviour from now on if he had any chance of winning her over.

'I'm sure tales of my younger days have been greatly exaggerated. Why don't you decide for yourself? You've made it clear you can think for yourself.'

'I suppose…' Her wary look began to falter.

'Why don't we start over? Have a clean slate?' It was likely the best chance he had of getting her on side if they were both able to set his past indiscretions aside. He'd never felt ashamed about his actions until now with Thaleia watching him, judging him, and so far finding him lacking in any moral fibre, it would seem.

Unfortunately, he couldn't dispute that quickly formed opinion, but he hoped he could change it in time. Perhaps if it got back to Alex that he'd treated her with respect, changed his ways, he might deem Enzo a friend again. Someone he wouldn't mind having around his son instead of keeping him at a distance.

He held out his hand, which Thaleia eventually shook, letting him breathe a sigh of relief.

'Perhaps I will take that tour after all, since we do have some time to kill.' There was a twinkle in Thaleia's eye as she spoke, showing that there was a sense of humour behind that brusque business manner.

Enzo had to admit that it wasn't what he'd expected Alex's sister to be like. Someone Alex had described to him as naïve and fanciful. She was the opposite, and he couldn't help but wonder if the change in her had come from her very public humiliation.

It was no wonder she wasn't in the mood for any games with a member of the opposite sex. He hadn't thought things through properly, otherwise he might have realised she'd had enough of men toying with her.

'It would be my pleasure, Ms Galatis.'

'Thaleia, please,' she said, letting him lead the way. A thaw hopefully beginning to set in between them.

'Thaleia it is, then.' Enzo knew she was likely as used to being on board a yacht as he was, and not as easily impressed as some of the young revellers he brought back from the nightclubs he frequented when he was ashore. However, he was still proud of *Bacchus* and had a sudden need for her to like it too. To be comfortable here.

For some reason he couldn't quite put his finger on at the moment, it was important to him that she validated his way of life. She wasn't a sycophant, there was no way she was going to be falling over herself, telling him things he wanted to hear. Thaleia told it how it was, and, so far, her review wasn't exactly a positive one.

He led her down towards the living quarters, thankful the deckhands had cleaned up after the last soirée on board. It had been a messy one as usual. He was just glad he had such an amazing crew who had the place shipshape in no time.

People didn't know when to stop when there was free food and booze, and often abused his hospitality. Not that he'd been in any state to care. When he was playing the gracious host, he liked to be in the thick of things. Often the instigator of the raucous drinking games that took place, resulting in something that looked like a crime scene the next morning. The rooms full of empty bottles, food mashed into the carpet, clothes strewn about, and usually half-naked bodies who slept where they'd eventually passed out. Carnage, yet he always made sure everyone went home happy. He didn't stand for any nonsense. This was a safe, fun place for all. Except, perhaps, himself.

When he was being the life and soul of the party, he didn't have to think about the fact he would rather be spending time with his sister, or his best friend. Finding out about the lives he was no longer a part of. It was in the cold light of day he was faced with his feelings of guilt and regret over the past. Perhaps that was why he'd been so keen to have Thaleia here for company. It was too bad that he'd yet again acted without thinking about the consequences.

'Is that a cinema screen?' Thaleia asked, spotting the pull-down projector screen mounted on the wall.

'Yes, well, it's not easy to get television reception out here so I find it easier to watch movies. The seats recline.'

'Of course they do,' she said, trailing her hand over the grey suede seats positioned for the perfect view. 'I suppose you have a popcorn cart somewhere too.'

'No, but I do like to dress up as an usher from time to time, selling ice creams during the interval.' He liked it when she smiled. It relaxed that frown that lined her forehead when she was talking to him.

'Now that, I would like to see.' She gave him a full-beam grin, which tugged at something deep inside him, and he found himself wanting more. If making fun of himself was the way to do it, he was willing to give it a try. After all, when he looked at all of this from an outsider's perspective, it was a tad ridiculous. Since his parents died, no one had been around to ever tell him no, and he'd taken advantage of that. Living his life like an unsupervised teenager. Which, in his heart, he still was, even if his body was that of a man in his mid-thirties. Albeit, one that swam every day in the ocean.

'Let me show you my study.' He managed to refrain from offering to role-play, but it wasn't easy for someone unused to having a filter. Instead, he steered away from the party room to the smaller, more private area he used when he simply wanted some alone time. Which wasn't often enough.

'This is somewhere I could quite happily spend my time.' Thaleia wandered around the room, reading the titles of the leather-bound books housed in his small library lining the shelves.

'You're a reader?'

'When I get the time. No offence, but I didn't have you down as the studious type.'

'Some taken,' he said, picking up the book he'd left open on his chair last night, and setting it to one side for later. 'I like to come in here in my downtime. It's supposed to be my office, but I do more actual work up top, rather than in here.'

'In your hot tub?'

'Sometimes. It's nicer to take video calls in the sun, rather than down here in the shadows.' She didn't have to know that there were times when he preferred that. Perhaps he was getting old when the frantic pace at which he led his life led to burnout now and again. Where he spent days, sometimes even weeks, at sea, simply reading, or watching old movies next door. On his own.

'I'm sure. Although you don't have to be at sea to do that. If you don't mind me asking, why live on a yacht? Especially when you could probably buy your own island if you wanted.'

'I get bored easily. I much prefer waking up and looking out at a different view on a regular basis.' For a long time that had included his bedroom habits too, but the meaningless flings left him feeling as though he were permanently part of a holiday romance. It had been great for a while, but he was beginning to tire of it. Bedding pretty women was fun but it was all style, no substance. He was no longer finding those brief hook-ups fulfilling. In fact, he'd enjoyed the lunch today with Thaleia more than any of his recent conquests.

He supposed Alex settling down into family life, taking care of his son, had made him wonder about the path he'd taken instead. These past years he'd almost been on a mission to prove his life was more fulfilling than being a responsible family man. However, Enzo was beginning to think he wasn't as happy as he'd thought.

Alex had a child he loved unconditionally, and no doubt that love was equally returned. Enzo hadn't had that since his parents died and it was possible he was harbouring some envy over that special relationship. One he hadn't managed to cultivate with his little sister when they'd both needed it. Considering how badly he'd messed that up, becoming a father wasn't something he craved.

Still, he wasn't ready to give all this up just yet. Even if there was a chance there might be a woman out there who could fill that void inside him where his family used to reside. Once upon a time he might have believed he could have it all. While that was true in terms of material possessions, losing his parents made him feel as though he'd lost everything. Their love, the relationship he'd had with them, was something he could never get back. And he'd ruined the chance of a proper relationship with Beatrice in failing her as a child. It was better for him to be on his own, no matter how lonely he sometimes felt. There was less chance of him, or anyone else, getting hurt.

'Hmm, some might say you were running from something.' The way she was studying him, seemed to see right inside his soul, made him nervous.

Enzo flopped down into his chair, suddenly tired of putting on a front. He was beginning to see he didn't have to do that around Thaleia. It was liberating, even if he wasn't about to spill all his deep dark secrets to her. 'I just enjoy living life, Thaleia. Perhaps one day I might decide to stay on dry land permanently, but not just yet.'

Thaleia stopped pacing the room and eventually sat down in a chair opposite with a huff of breath. 'I guess I'm doing the opposite. I thought I was going to settle down, but I'm sure you know how that turned out. It's been well documented.'

Enzo gave a brief nod so she knew she didn't have to go into details of her heartbreak.

'Anyway, I decided to get away from everything. I want to live my own life without relying on a partner, my parents, or anyone else. That's why making my business a success is so important to me.'

Enzo admired that. It had taken courage to walk away from that luxury life to carve out some independence. Something he'd never done. Instead, choosing to live off his parents' legacy. Oh, he was still part of the company in name, but everyone else made the big decisions and he simply collected the cheques at the end. He hadn't had to use the degree he'd worked for when everything was done for him.

'I'm glad I can bring a little business your way.' He wanted to help her when she appeared to have isolated herself on this island away from everyone else. No doubt licking the wounds left from her ex-fiancé.

Enzo understood that need for distance when he'd been doing it for over a decade. Though he'd surrounded himself with strangers to stop from feeling lonely. He wasn't sure how Thaleia was managing it. If she was.

'It's appreciated. If I haven't said it yet, thank you. I know you could have taken your business elsewhere and been given a warmer reception.' Thaleia's little smile as she poked fun at herself was a pleasant sight to see, and he hoped that going forward their relationship would run a little smoother. Not least because he had a favour to ask of her.

Now that it appeared he'd grown on her a little, he was hoping she could help him out with something that wasn't usually a problem. 'That's true, and I'm willing to forgive and forget—'

'That's very magnanimous of you, Enzo.'

'As I was saying, I'm prepared to forgive and

forget, *if* you could do something for me in return.'

'What?' There was that wary look again. It seemed as though she was always waiting, anticipating an ulterior motive for getting her here. That might have been true of women he'd brought here in the past, but he genuinely enjoyed her company. That was what had put the idea in his head to ask her in the first place.

'This party I'm going to requires a plus one, and, before you ask, yes, it is a necessity, otherwise I'll have everyone trying to matchmake on my behalf. And before you say no, there will be no strings attached. It will save me the trouble of having to find someone else.'

'Charming.'

'You're a very confusing woman, Thaleia. I thought you didn't want me to see you as anything other than a business associate.' If she'd shown any interest in anything more he would have had to seriously remind himself of the pact he'd made with Alex. Flirting was one thing, but crossing that line would have serious repercussions.

'I don't, but that doesn't mean I want to be seen as a mere convenience either.'

Enzo would never understand women. Certainly not this one, it would seem. 'I just meant you'd be doing me a favour, nothing more. If I asked someone else, well, they might read more into it. I know you don't owe me anything but it could be a good opportunity for you to network. I'll certainly spread the word about your business, and hopefully, if the guest of honour wears my gift, you'll get a lot of interest and future business.'

His idea of dating was limited to restaurants and clubs, with the occasional sleepover on the yacht. Inviting a random woman to this high-profile gathering might give the wrong impression, and he wasn't in the market for anything serious. If he could get Thaleia to agree, it would save him a lot of trouble. Plus, he didn't have to put on a show. He could relax and be himself around her, safe in the knowledge that she had no interest in him. At least that would keep Alex happy if he ever found out they'd spent time together.

'Can you give me some time to think it over?'

'Sure.' He was surprised she was even considering it and wasn't going to pressure her for an answer.

'I take it there's a strict dress code.'

'I imagine it won't be a formal affair, but you know the score. Dress to impress.' That meant flaunting the wealth. Something he'd been happy to do before now, but he knew Thaleia wasn't going to be impressed by expensive designer gear. Usually he didn't care what people thought of him, but for some reason, her opinion mattered.

'I know all too well the kind of party it will be. It's more about being seen than actually being there.'

'Right, but you can use that to your advantage. Of course, I'll cover any costs for your outfit. Just let me know what you have in mind.'

'Don't worry about that. I'm sure I have plenty of suitable gowns. They won't get much wear out here.' It was already beginning to sound as though it was a foregone conclusion that she would be going with him, but Enzo didn't push the matter. If she decided it was in her best interests to accompany him, all the better.

'I'll leave that down to you. Well, it looks as though we're back to where we started.' He pointed out of the window to where they could see the island again. Although they were getting along better now, and she was thinking about helping him out, he wasn't used to people invading his personal space. Yes, he'd invited her in, but he'd almost relaxed too much, given more of himself away to her than anyone else. He'd never shared his private study before or planned an introduction to one of his friends. Thaleia Galatis had breached his defences in a matter of just hours and he'd be glad to get back a little space.

To compose himself, and get back to the Enzo Capelli who didn't need anyone else in his life.

'Oh. Good. I'll have to get back to work.' Thaleia jumped up, as though she too had somehow let her guard down, and they both hurried back on deck.

Once the ship was anchored they were able to launch the tender and one of his crew would take her back. Enzo helped her down into the boat, part of him wanting to get in with her and sail away. A ridiculous notion when he barely knew her, and she'd only just stopped looking at him as though he were the devil incarnate. But there was something about her that made him feel at peace. That made him want to stop running away from the real world. All the more reason to send her away.

'Thank you for coming, and I'm sorry again for taking you away from your work. Also, for not reporting me to the police for kidnapping.'

'I'm still considering that one,' she said with a grin. 'I'll let you know my decision tomorrow. On everything.'

Enzo watched her sail away until she was nothing more than a speck in the distance. Regardless that Thaleia was completely off limits to him, he was already looking forward to seeing, and speaking to, her again. A novelty to him when usually his interest in the opposite sex was based on a physical attraction only. Although the connection between them, through Alex, and the fact she was now working for Enzo, should have prevented him from pursuing further contact, he knew nothing could happen between them, so she was safe, even if she was already making him break all his own rules.

CHAPTER THREE

'DO YOU HAVE enough money, Thaleia?' Helena Galatis peered closer at the screen.

Thaleia had made the video call while sitting outside enjoying her breakfast, keen to get the weekly check-in over with. 'Yes, Mother.'

'Are you eating? You look skinny.'

'Yes, I'm eating. See?' Thaleia held her piece of avocado toast up to the phone. She knew none of her family thought she could make this work, but that only made her all the more determined to succeed.

'I want you to look pretty for our anniversary party in two weeks' time. All the best people will be there, and you might catch the eye of a nice Greek boy if you're lucky.'

Thaleia sighed. What her mother meant was that all the richest people she knew, and those she wanted to know, would be there. It was pointless telling her mother she wasn't interested in finding another man because she wouldn't understand. To her parents, marrying into the right family was more important than anything. Even this anniversary party they were hosting was more about the people attending than actually celebrating their marriage. Thaleia wanted more than that, and if she couldn't find it she'd rather be on her own. She didn't relish an evening being paraded around like livestock for the highest bidder.

Slowly, a plan formed in her mind. Enzo wanted her to do him a favour by being his plus one, and perhaps he could do her one in return.

'Actually, I've already met someone. It's early days but I think you'll like him.' It was a bit premature since she hadn't got Enzo to agree to anything but at least it would get her mother off her case for now and hopefully prevent her from creating a list of suitors she was supposed to entertain at the party.

'Oh? Who are his family?' The most important question, obviously. Not 'what is he like?', 'where did you meet?' or the normal questions anyone else would ask. Basically, she wanted the low-down on if he was worth knowing.

Thaleia cleared her throat. This might be easier if her parents hadn't heard of Enzo before now. 'It's Enzo Capelli, Mother. Alex's friend from university.'

The silence was deafening, and she worried she'd gone too far.

'Of the Capelli Shipping fortune?' Of course, it wasn't the man's history, but his bank account that interested her mother. For once, that worked in Thaleia's favour.

'Yes. He lives on a yacht but he's staying near the island. I'm accompanying him to Irida's party next week.' Since Thaleia wanted a favour from him now, she guessed that meant the decision was made.

'Oh. How lovely. That's the biggest event in the social calendar. He sounds like a good one, Thaleia, don't mess this one up. I can't wait to meet him.'

Thaleia restrained from rolling her eyes, a habit she was often scolded for when it gave away exactly what she was thinking without saying a word. Instead, she steered the conversation in a different direction.

'Will Alex be at your anniversary party?'

Her mother pursed her lips. 'He won't, unfortunately. We've invited him but he says he's busy with Georgios. As if we wouldn't want to see our own grandson.'

'He's only a boy. I'm sure it's not the kind of event Alex wants him to attend. He'll bring him when he's ready, Mother.' Thaleia was proud of her brother, though on this occasion it was probably for the best he didn't turn up. His relationship with their parents was strained, and she saw little of him these days. He'd only brought little Georgios to see the family once in Athens.

It wouldn't improve relations if he thought she was hooked up with his best friend. Alex had warned her about him enough and she didn't want to have to go through the humiliation of explaining the situation. Especially since she hadn't even asked Enzo if he would agree to this charade. Though she wouldn't worry too much about Alex finding out through their parents. Contact was limited between them and since he'd already said he wouldn't be attending it wasn't likely they'd be discussing the party again.

'Yes, well, you know your brother. He's always busy. Anyway, I must go. If Enzo Capelli is coming to the party I might have to buy myself a new dress. I'll talk to you later, sweetie.' Her mother blew her a kiss but ended the call before Thaleia had a chance to say goodbye.

It was no wonder Alex was keeping his distance these days when their parents seemed so self-absorbed. If it wasn't their father boasting about some new business deal, it was their mother's endless talk about who she'd met and what she was wearing. Thaleia had no doubt she'd already spent a fortune on some bespoke dress for the occasion, but that wouldn't stop her shopping again now she had someone else to impress.

Thaleia didn't begrudge them the lives they led, she simply wished they'd let her and Alex get on with theirs without interference.

She turned her phone off and set it on the table. Once she finished her orange juice she'd get back to work. The piece she'd created had given her a new burst of life. A feeling of accomplishment, at knowing it was going to be worn, and seen at such a high-profile event. Hopefully.

She'd started work immediately after coming ashore yesterday. Perhaps partly to try and forget the time she'd spent with Enzo, but also because she was keen to see the finished piece herself. The lunch on his yacht had been eye-opening. Not so much because of the illustrious location, but because she'd got to see a little of the man behind the legend. It was that man—the one who read quietly on his own, who apologised for his behaviour—who was occupying her thoughts.

Until this morning she'd thought she would refuse his invitation on those grounds alone. Spending more time with him, getting to know him better, and perhaps even liking him, could prove detrimental to the content life she'd made for herself here. However, having him with her at her parents' anniversary party was preferable to the speed dating her mother would inevitably set up for her over the course of the evening. At least she knew who she was dealing with where Enzo was concerned, and he was no more interested in settling down than she was in being a casual fling. This arrangement might just suit them both, as long as she didn't fall for his charms along the way and get herself into more trouble.

'Good morning.' The sound of the man himself made her jump.

'Enzo? I wasn't expecting you this morning.' She pulled her silk dressing gown a little tighter over her camisole. It wasn't usual to see anyone at this time of the day, so she never thought twice about having breakfast in her nightwear. Or without putting her make-up on, or brushing her hair. She was suddenly self-conscious and feeling a little bit vulnerable to be caught unaware like this.

'Sorry. I didn't mean to intrude on your breakfast. I can leave and call back another time.' Perhaps sensing that she was a tad uncomfortable, he turned to go, but it was obvious he'd come all this way to discuss something. Besides, sending him away would seem churlish, and she needed him to agree to the new plan.

'It's fine. Take a seat.' Thaleia pointed to the chair opposite. It wasn't quite the same as the last time they'd sat at a table, but she believed the view was just as spectacular when they could see over the cliffs and down to the sea. The blues and greens she'd come to love so much.

'Thanks.' He didn't take much persuading and was soon helping himself to a slice of toast.

'Can I get you some juice, or coffee?'

'Coffee, please. I didn't stop for breakfast this morning.'

Thaleia poured him out a small cup of coffee and sat back, keen to find out what had brought him here this morning. She certainly didn't have him figured for an early riser, more like someone who didn't let sleep get in the way of his partying at all. Except he was perfectly groomed and wasn't wearing yesterday's clothes as she might have expected of someone of his reputation.

'So what brings you ashore at this hour? Or is this the morning after the night before?' She couldn't resist a tease. Although there was a tinge of something bitter in her mouth as she said the words, imagining him spending a night with someone else on the island. Shivers made their way up her neck as she realised the implications of that thought. She had absolutely no need to feel put out even if that was the case. If they did agree to be one another's fake dates, it still didn't give either of them a right to feel possessive.

That way lay madness, and heartbreak. She'd

been there and didn't have the strength to set up somewhere else to get over a failed romance. And why was she even thinking about this? *Aargh!*

'I have some business nearby, but I thought I'd take the opportunity to drop in and see if you'd come to a decision about the party. I know, I know, I said I wouldn't pressure you, but if you decide not to attend I'll have to find someone else.'

'A terrible chore, I'm sure,' she teased. No doubt the selection process involved some of the local clubs and Enzo propping up the bar waiting for every pretty girl that passed his way.

'You really don't have a high opinion of me, do you? If you remember, you were my first choice, Thaleia.'

'Out of convenience,' she reminded him, not knowing why that still niggled when she barely knew the man beyond his reputation. Perhaps it was a hangover from her fiancé leaving her for any other woman he could find.

Enzo leaned across the table and held her gaze, his voice a low whisper. 'Trust me, you were my first choice for more reason than that.'

Then he sat back in his seat and sipped his coffee nonchalantly, as though he hadn't just turned her insides into a washing machine. She'd experienced more heat in that look and the sound of his voice than she'd felt in months.

A deep breath and a reminder that she couldn't afford to let him sweet-talk her and she managed to recompose herself. 'Anyway, I've thought it over and I'll agree on one condition.'

'Name it. Anything you want.'

'My parents are having an anniversary party—'

Enzo threw his hands up. 'Nope. No way.'

'You said anything.'

'Within reason. I don't do "meet the family" scenarios, and I'm pretty sure your brother wouldn't be happy to see me there with you.'

'This is different. For a start, we're not together. I just need someone to stop my mother pairing me off with random men.'

'You want me to be your arm candy?' he said with a smirk.

'No. Yes. Whatever it takes to stop my mother trying to marry me off again. I'm not interested, but she doesn't want to hear that. It will be easier if she just thinks we're together.'

'And your brother?'

They both knew Alex wouldn't be happy whether he knew this was a set-up or not. 'He's already told Mother he won't be coming and I'm certainly not going to tell him you're coming as my date.'

She could do without any lectures on getting

involved with the wrong man. Goodness knew she'd given herself a good talking-to after her ex. This arrangement would be a favour and nothing more.

'And if I agree, you'll come to Irida's party with me?'

Thaleia took a deep breath, feeling very much as though she were agreeing to sell her soul to the devil. 'Yes.'

Instead of jumping right in, or shaking her hand to seal the deal, Enzo stroked his chin. Looking every inch a villain coming up with a cunning plan. 'Then you must be quite desperate for my company at your parents' anniversary. That puts me in a very interesting position.'

She should have known this would come at a price. He wasn't the sort of man to do something for nothing. Especially when he appeared to be the one holding all the power. 'Just forget it. I'm not going to compromise myself.'

She stood up from the table, ready to walk away from the whole thing. As she turned away, Enzo grabbed her by thc hand, forcing her to turn and look at him. He was standing so near, she took an intake of breath, not prepared to be so close to him.

'I wouldn't ask you to do that, Thaleia. I'm not the monster you think I am. I'm sorry. I was just teasing. Please forgive me. I didn't mean to upset you.'

'What is it you do want, Enzo?' She was weary of always feeling on the back foot when she was around him. Not so much because of what he said or did, but because her body apparently didn't see him as the threat her mind did.

His touch, his voice, his fresh, spicy scent gave her heart palpitations, along with a curiosity about what it would be like to spend the night on that yacht with him. She was a woman, after all, and not as immune to his charms as she'd hoped.

It was his turn to look perturbed. 'To spend time with you. I don't mean in the way you probably think. I'm not a complete sleaze. I just mean I enjoy your company. I don't have many people I can call real friends and I liked having someone to really talk to yesterday. I get the impression you're kind of isolated here too and I thought perhaps, while I'm here, we could enjoy some time together.'

'I have a lot of work to do.' It was the only excuse her mind could conjure when every other part of her was screaming, telling her to jump at the chance to be with him.

'I know, and I don't want to get in the way of that. I thought perhaps I could come and see you on your lunch break. Bring a picnic. In return, you could show me around the island. That doesn't sound too heinous, does it?'

'I guess not…' There didn't seem any reason to refuse when he was offering to do something nice for her, and she really needed him to come to this party. Besides, she had enjoyed his company too—that was what had her worried so much.

'That's settled, then. I'll let you get on with your work. I've taken up too much of your time already, and I have some people to see. I'll come by tomorrow, about twelve o'clock?'

'Make it half past twelve,' she said, trying to wrest back a little bit of control.

'I'll see you then.' He gave her a nod and walked away, whistling.

Thaleia sat down and watched him walk away, wondering what on earth she'd got herself into this time.

Enzo couldn't help but smile, even though he wasn't proud that he'd told a little white lie to Thaleia. Last night he hadn't been able to settle at all. Snippets of their conversation and visions of Thaleia filling his head. Usually, his go-to in this sort of situation would be to go and find a curvy substitute to keep his mind and body busy. Except the thought of getting ready for a night out on the tiles hadn't been as appealing as usual. He blamed Thaleia and her disapproving look. The one he was sure she'd give him if she were to witness him in action.

So, he'd stayed in and tortured himself with thoughts of the one woman he knew he couldn't have. Not only because she wasn't interested, but also because her brother would kill him. He'd headed inland first thing this morning just so he could see her. There were no business meetings or anything else pulling him here. The very thought laughable to someone who delegated that sort of responsibility to others. He'd simply wanted an excuse to see her again. The sight of her just awake, in her nightwear, wasn't going to help him forget about her. Imagining how she'd look in his bed, next to him, her hair in disarray as it had been this morning.

Yes, Alex would definitely kill him if he knew just how much Enzo was taken by his little sister.

CHAPTER FOUR

'CAN I SEE IT?'

'I don't usually show people what I'm working on until it's finished.' Thaleia bit her lip as she denied Enzo's request. She was always self-conscious about showing people her work until she was completely satisfied with it in case they didn't like it, or showed their displeasure in some way, making her doubt her own capabilities. Her judgement wasn't always the best, as proven by a fiancé who'd left her on their wedding day.

'I understand. No problem.' Enzo had arrived dead on time, picnic basket slung over his arm, just as he'd promised. She'd got so caught up in what she was doing it was she who'd forgotten the time, so he'd caught her just finishing up when she'd planned to have the pendant out of sight until it was ready.

Except she couldn't ignore the look of disappointment on his face. 'Well, maybe just a little look. There's a long way to go until it's finished, but it's beginning to take shape.'

She set the pendant in his hand, and he turned it over in his palm, inspecting it with such interest she was worried he'd found a flaw.

'I love the curves. It really represents the ocean. And the sparkle certainly catches your eye.' His praise gave her a confidence boost that she was on the right track after all, as long as the recipient appreciated it just as much as Enzo.

'Diamonds will do that,' she laughed, though it meant getting the symmetry right was imperative. A millimetre out between the settings in the multiple curves and it would be obvious.

'The sapphires are just as pretty, and equally effective. I'm sure Irida is going to be over the moon about it. I'll let you put it somewhere safe in the meantime.' Enzo handed the expensive work in progress back to her so she could secure it in her safe until they returned. Although there weren't that many people around, she still had to be security conscious when the shop was full of expensive stock. Not least this piece, which she couldn't afford to leave lying around for anyone to find.

Once she'd secured the pendant, she did a last check of her make-up and hair and went back to Enzo's side. 'So, where are we going?'

'I thought you could tell me. You're supposed to be giving me a tour. I'm just providing refreshments.' He tapped the wicker basket he'd picked up again.

'It depends if you want a history tour, or just want to enjoy the scenery.' She hadn't given it too much thought, her mind more occupied with what she was going to wear after he'd seen her at her worst now on two occasions.

It wasn't that she wanted to impress him necessarily, but she wanted to feel as though she looked good at least. In the end she'd settled on a white cotton, strappy dress embellished with lemons. A summery, bright choice, which definitely would not have met the dress code for either of the parties they were to attend. Perhaps that was why she felt so comfortable in it.

'I don't want to give you any more work. I'm happy to simply go somewhere nice where we can spread out the picnic blanket and enjoy our lunch.' From the outside it would seem that Enzo was doing her a favour, but all that was on Thaleia's mind was that it would be more intimate if they weren't mingling with tourists at the local spots of historical interest.

It also meant there would be more talking involved, and, while she was keen to find out more about him, she was worried about getting too close. Especially when they had a couple of social engagements to navigate together, hopefully without incident.

'Why don't we go to the beach? I know a little place, sheltered from the wind.' It wasn't too far away and it was somewhere she was comfortable being. Her happy place away from the shop when she had time to sit with a book, or simply do a little sun worshipping. When she was feeling brave she even ventured into the water.

She wasn't the best swimmer in the world, but out here where no one could see her, she liked to have a dip in the sea. It was invigorating for body and soul and had done wonders for her peace of mind since coming here. When she was out there, she didn't worry about her family, or her ex, or even the business. She simply enjoyed the moment. Something she needed to do a lot more of. She needed to be more Enzo.

'Sounds perfect. Lead on.' Enzo popped his shades on to protect his stunning eyes from the sun and followed her down the pathway from the shop.

Familiar with the steep incline, she chose to remove her cord wedges before making her way down the beach. Enzo on the other hand was struggling to stay upright, his fancy white trainers getting messed up as he slid and stumbled his way down.

'Would you like me to take the basket?' she asked, pretending she wasn't enjoying seeing him on the back foot for a change.

'Thank you.' His face was dark, that grin she was used to seeing lost in his discomfort. Until eventually he grew tired of sliding his way down the sand and grass and pulled his shoes off. Hopping on one foot, he grabbed one trainer and lobbed it down onto the sand, closely followed by the other. 'That's better.'

'More money than sense,' Thaleia muttered, before fetching his now sand-covered trainers and dusting them off.

'Thanks.' He took his trainers back, but set them down on the sand again, remaining barefoot.

'Far be it from me to criticise, Enzo, but you do seem to live quite a wasteful life.' It was only since she moved to the island for a simpler existence that she realised she'd done the same. She'd had everything money could buy, and more, but it hadn't made her happy. It was only by stripping away everything that had been handed to her, and starting over, building her own business and life away from the family, that she'd found contentment. Maybe he needed to do the same. To take a step back from the luxury and see that there was a different way of life. Or at least appreciate what he had, and what others didn't.

She waited for him to kick off. Certainly her father would have if anyone had ever dared criticise him in any shape or form. In the end, Enzo simply shrugged.

‘I know. It’s been that way since my parents died. Who knows? Perhaps I’m trying to fill the void they left with material things and people I hardly know, but I doubt I’m going to change now.’ It was surprisingly frank for a man of his status, basically admitting that none of it brought him true joy. He was simply trying to find something to keep him busy. A bit like her coming out here. She wondered once again what it was that he was running from.

‘You do still have some family though, don’t you? A sister?’

He nodded. ‘Beatrice. There is a ten-year age gap between us, so we’re not exactly close.’

‘She must have been young when your parents died.’ Some quick mental arithmetic told her that his little sister couldn’t have been more than a child when she was orphaned. It was difficult to understand why they wouldn’t be close if they only had each other. Unless this was the thing he’d been avoiding while continually at sea.

‘She was. We both were. I was much too young to have responsibility for her. She went to boarding school in England while I was at university so we probably didn’t see enough of one another. It made her very independent, having to grow up so quickly. She’s likely much more mature than I am.' There was that self-deprecating humour again and Thaleia was beginning to suspect he used it to deflect attention away from any real emotion.

'You could have taken her to the party.' It would have saved him a lot of bother, even if it would leave her in the lurch when it came to her family.

'I'm not sure she would have been any more willing to accompany me than you were,' he said with a heavy sigh. 'I'm afraid she might not have a very high opinion of me either.'

'That's a shame if you've only got each other left.' Sometimes she wished she had Alex living closer so she had someone to talk to, but she knew he had his hands full with Georgios. She supposed even before then, when he was running as wild as Enzo, Alex had never really had time for her. Not since they were children. Back then it had felt as though it was just the two of them against the world. Then it became Alex against their father. Then he was gone. Off to university and hardly heard from again.

It was easy to lose contact if there wasn't an effort made to maintain it, even in families. With Enzo's sister growing up in boarding school, Thaleia supposed it was only natural that they'd drifted apart too. Although, in this instance, it seemed very much as though Enzo was afraid to get in touch with his sibling now in case she rejected him. Thaleia knew a little about how that felt. How it was easier to hide away than put yourself out there, feeling vulnerable in case it happened again. She got the impression neither of them was in the market for a serious relationship of any kind.

'She has her life, teaching in Switzerland, and I have mine, on the yacht. That's just the way it is. Now, what would you like to drink? I have a nice bottle of white wine, some sparkling water or lemonade.' Enzo busied himself spreading out the picnic blanket and the contents of the basket. Clearly uncomfortable talking about the subject, and she didn't want to spoil the moment when he'd gone to so much trouble.

'Just a lemonade for me. I want to keep a clear head while I'm working. Sharp tools and alcohol don't go well together.' Even after the wine she'd had yesterday things had seemed a little hazy for a while and the file had slipped a few times when she'd been trying to shape the metal. She was lucky she'd suffered only a few cuts, but she didn't want the same thing happening today. Not when she'd be working with a soldering iron and high heat.

'Perhaps I'll take a leaf out of your book too, and just have a lemonade for a change.' Enzo poured out two glasses from the flip-top bottle, and helped himself to some of the feta and yogurt pita bites he'd laid out. He was lying lengthways on the blanket, more at home than Thaleia, who was sitting with her knees drawn up on the edge of it, not comfortable enough yet to lie down next to him.

'Oh? Is all of that partying catching up with you? I imagine it does take a toll.'

He gave her an unimpressed look. 'No. I'm simply taking it easy today. I can live without alcohol and partying, you know.'

'Really? You do surprise me.' She took a bite out of an apple, relishing the teasing. Despite her reluctance to get too cosy with him, there was an ease between them when it came to conversation. It wasn't stilted or awkward, as though they'd known each other for most of their lives.

'I do have other interests,' he insisted.

'Like?'

'I have my business.'

'Which other people seem to run for you or else you wouldn't be sailing around on a yacht without a care in the world.'

'I like reading, and I can cook, believe it or not. It's just good manners to let the chef on board do his job and stay out of the kitchen.'

'Uh-huh.' A smile played on her lips.

'If you don't believe me, maybe I'll cook something for you.'

'I'll believe it when I see it.' The food was all so lovely and fresh here she didn't believe for one moment that he had anything to do with it other than carry it ashore.

'I will. I'll cook at your place once all of this is over. Before I head back out into the big wide ocean.' It should have been the mention of them being in the close confines of her villa that got her tied up in knots. Instead it was the mention of him leaving that didn't sit well with her.

Although they hadn't spent a lot of time together, they had plans to, and she was getting used to him calling in unannounced. She had a feeling she was going to miss him when he was gone.

'There will come a time when partying with bikini-clad girls does start to look a bit tragic.' Her defence against any feelings that threatened to make their way towards him was to keep the banter going between them. He could easily point out how tragic her life was, hiding out on an island after being jilted at the altar, and she had to be prepared for that too. Although, these past few days she didn't seem to be dwelling on it as much as she usually did. Likely because her head was full of Enzo and parties. Everything that was currently giving her heart palpitations at present.

'I think I can live with that. Although, I'm

quite content here.' He turned over onto his back, hands behind his head, and closed his eyes.

Thaleia took a moment to study him. He really was a handsome man. Those long dark lashes would be the envy of many women, not to mention those kissable lips…

When she glanced back up, it was to find him watching her.

She cleared her throat and brushed the sand from her dress. 'It is a lovely spot. I like to come here in my downtime. It reminds me of the times Alex and I used to play on the beach when we were little. I was always a little afraid of the sea. It seemed so big and deep. Alex would hold my hand and we would play this game, jumping over the waves as they crashed onto the shore. We were only paddling in the shallows really, but it got me over my fear.'

It was a memory that had just occurred to her. They had been close once. Her big brother looking out for her, helping her, instead of making fun of her the way some might have done. Although she missed that bond, Georgios needed him more as a father. She simply wished she had someone in her life who was there to keep her right and steer her clear of danger.

Thaleia dug her toes into the sand, trying to recapture the moment, and failing.

'Do you swim now?' Enzo sat up beside her.

'Not very well, but I do like to come here, where there's no one else around.'

Enzo suddenly got on his feet and held his hand out to her. 'Why don't we go for a dip now?'

'I don't think so.'

'Well, I'm game, even if you're not.' With that, Enzo tugged off his shirt and ran straight into the sea, letting out a few expletives as the cool water reached all parts of him.

He did make her laugh, she'd give him that. The view wasn't bad either. He was making a habit of stripping off in front of her and she wasn't going to scold him for it. Even if she'd no intention of undressing herself, Thaleia did venture down to the edge of the sea to paddle. Enzo waved at her from out in the sea, every now and then, rolling onto his back and floating effortlessly on the surface. This was the peace she thought they'd both been searching for. It was a shame it couldn't last. Once they left this cove, she had to go back to work, and Enzo would return to his yacht and whoever he chose to join him there next.

Enzo had begun swimming back to her when he suddenly disappeared below the water. When he resurfaced, he was spluttering and clutching his chest. Thaleia's heart was in her mouth. She was worried that he'd suffered some sort of medical emergency when they were miles away from help.

'Is everything OK?' she called out.

Enzo gave her a thumbs up, which had to suffice until he was back on his feet and walking towards her. Water snaking down his naked torso, and his shorts riding low on his hips, showing off that sexy muscle line at either side that made her weak at the knees.

'Jelly fish, I think.' He pointed to a red mark on his flat stomach but otherwise didn't seem too perturbed about it.

'Perhaps we should get you back.'

'I'll live. Come on, you've still some time left on your lunch break.' He took her hand and guided her into the water swirling onto the already wet sand.

As the waves rolled in, he jumped over them, into the foam, pulling her with him. Until they were crying with laughter, and the bottom half of her dress was soaked with seawater. She didn't think she'd ever feel this carefree again. Especially not with someone holding her hand. It was nice. Comforting. Dangerous. Enzo was someone she was able to relax and enjoy herself with. Making her feel lighter than she had in months. A seductive position to find herself in, regardless that it could never go anywhere.

Then Enzo let go of her hand. As the water

crashed in around their ankles she could tell something was wrong by the frown on his face.

'What's wrong, Enzo?'

'I don't know. I've just started shaking. Something doesn't feel right.'

'It could be a reaction to the jellyfish sting. Let's get you back to my place.' She knew that if he had a serious reaction to the sting they could be in trouble out here.

He let her lead him out of the water, and she shook the sand off the blanket, using it as a makeshift towel to dry him off. Trying her best not to ogle him when she could feel him trembling beneath her fingers.

'We need to get you warmed up. Put this on.' She handed him his shirt back, but his hands were shaking so much he couldn't manage by himself and had to rely on her assistance.

He was uncharacteristically quiet, and she made the decision to leave the lunch things where they were. It was more important to get him treated. She would come back later to collect everything. Taking his hand in hers, she led him back up the hill to her place. Rushing him inside and sitting him down while she collected some fresh towels.

'Get those wet things off, and wrap yourself up in these,' she commanded, turning away as he stepped out of his wet shorts and wrapped a towel around his waist.

'You can be very bossy, Thaleia Galatis,' he said as she fussed around him again, making sure he was wrapped up.

'I just don't want you dying before you've paid me,' she joshed, trying to lighten the mood.

'I wouldn't dare.'

She fetched him a glass of water, then returned when she'd found some antihistamines. 'This should help your reaction to the sting. Open up.'

Enzo opened his mouth and she popped the pill into it, before lifting the glass up so he could wash it down with some water.

'Thanks. I'm already feeling much better.' There was something in the tone of his voice, in the way that he was looking at her, that changed the atmosphere between them.

Thaleia was suddenly feeling all hot and bothered, realising just how close to him she was standing, and that he was practically naked. She did her best not to let it show, even though there was a hitch in her breath as she spoke.

'That's good. Glad I could help.'

Caught in some sort of invisible trap, she couldn't seem to move away. Their eyes locked in an unspoken agreement about what was going to happen next.

His lips met hers, hard and fast. The passion

almost knocking her off her feet. His hand at her waist, pulling her towards him, kept her upright for the moment, though Thaleia was melting against him. A kiss she hadn't expected, and no doubt would come to regret, but which she was very much enjoying. Enzo was as confident and capable in his technique as he was in every other area of his life, it would seem.

All too soon the moment was over. He released her, leaving her head in a spin and her legs weak. 'Sorry. That shouldn't have happened. Blame the shock. Please don't let this spoil things. I'll let you get back to work.'

Before she could process what had happened, or what was happening, Enzo was pulling his wet clothes back on in a hurry.

'Are you sure you'll be OK to go back?' Although she hadn't had time to process everything, she still didn't want him putting himself in jeopardy over one kiss. Albeit one passionate, moreish kiss she'd been sorry had ended.

'I'll be fine. Thanks for everything, and sorry again.' He stopped short of promising not to mix business and pleasure in future, and Thaleia was glad. Though she wasn't sure how she felt at that moment, she did know she didn't want him to disappear for ever.

Enzo hurried out of the villa, barefoot, half dressed, and wet. Looking for all the world as though he'd just been caught by a lover's husband and had to make a quick exit.

Chance would be a fine thing. Thaleia surprised herself with that thought. She didn't want a fling with anyone, much less a known playboy. Yet he'd awakened something inside her that she had a feeling wasn't going to be easily forgotten.

She'd wanted that kiss, and more. A shiver crept along her skin as she recalled how it felt to be swept into his arms and feel his desire for her in that moment. Intoxicating. Yet she knew in the long run it was better that he had ended it. They still had business to complete together, as well as functions to attend. It would be awful if things between them became suddenly awkward and tense when they'd begun to get along so well. Too well, it seemed. They'd become so comfortable together there had been a lapse in concentration for both of them. Thaleia was sure it was the drama of the moment that had caused them to forget themselves. The close quarters, along with her simply trying to be there for him, had conspired to conjure a false sense of intimacy between them. One best forgotten.

She picked up the damp towels he'd discarded in haste and deposited them in the laundry basket. They smelled of the sea, and of Enzo. It was all she could do not to wrap them around her and inhale his scent, imagining she was back in his embrace. Had it really been that long since someone held her, touched her, that she was clinging to the memory of a moment of madness?

She supposed finding out a man thought her attractive enough to kiss had simply gone to her head after her ex's rejection had all but killed her self-confidence. As long as she didn't get carried away thinking it was anything more than an ill-timed, misjudged lapse of common sense, there would be no harm done.

Even if she could still feel his hands imprinted on her waist, the taste of him burning on her lips, and the effect he'd had on the rest of her body was taking its time dissipating. It had been a startling reminder that she was still very much alive, even if a part of her had died at the altar that fateful day. Despite the broken heart, and humiliation, she still had wants and needs. It just wasn't a good idea to direct them towards Enzo.

If she began to feel the need for a partner again, it would be someone who wanted the same things she did in a relationship. To settle down and have a family. Things Enzo had never pretended were part of his agenda.

The bell in the shop rang and Thaleia was glad of the distraction. She hurried through to find her neighbour standing there.

'Agathi? Is everything OK? I missed you this morning.' The old woman wasn't carrying her usual cart full of goodies, and, though Thaleia had no appetite, it was unusual to see Agathi without her wares.

'I came to tell you my friend's husband passed away. I've spent the morning with her. It's a terrible business.' She dabbed her eyes with a tissue, visibly distressed by the events.

'How awful. What happened?'

'Konstantin died in his sleep. He was only eighty-nine.'

Thaleia understood the woman's upset, regardless that the man had clearly lived a full life. The Mediterranean diet, the sea, and sun, and the general lifestyle here, meant that most of the island's occupants lived to a ripe old age. They were certainly all still very active. Like most men around here, she supposed, he had been one of the fishermen who made their living here.

'I'm so sorry. It's clearly been a shock. Would you like to come in and sit down? Can I get you a drink?'

'No. I have to do my rounds and explain to people why I've let them down.'

'I'm sure that could wait until tomorrow. People will understand. You have to take care of yourself too, Agathi.'

'I'll feel better explaining, and passing on the news about Konstantin. Now, that's the bad news. I need some good news. Who was that handsome young man who came sprinting out of your house half undressed? I hope I didn't disturb anything?'

Thaleia's face felt as though it were in flames. She shouldn't have been surprised by Agathi's straightforward manner, but being expected to recount what had happened had got her hot all over again.

'No. Of course not. He's a customer. An acquaintance of my family's. We were down in the cove and he was stung by a jellyfish. He was simply here so I could treat the sting.' Fine job she'd done as a nurse, kissing her patient when he was likely in shock. Her shame burned brighter.

Agathi's pale blue eyes burned into her, her mouth tilted up at one side. 'Really? Did you have to give him mouth-to-mouth resuscitation? Is that why your lipstick was all over him?'

Thaleia's hand flew straight to her mouth as she imagined she too had lipstick smudged all around her face after their passionate kiss. Only to remember she wasn't wearing any. Agathi was a sly old fox.

'There's nothing to be ashamed of, my dear. You're too young and beautiful to hide yourself away out here. Go, have fun, kiss handsome boys. Life is too short.' With those words of wisdom, Agathi left the villa. No doubt to spread her bad, and good, news wherever else she travelled.

Thaleia knew Agathi was just reacting to the death of a friend, but it also gave her some pause for thought. She had been having fun with Enzo as they ate lunch, paddled in the sea, and especially when they kissed. The world hadn't ended. At least not yet.

She didn't want to live to eighty-nine on her own, without ever experiencing the joy of being with someone again, of having family around her. Today had given her an insight as to how that would feel. When Enzo had taken her hand and splashed in the sea with her, he'd reawakened the old Thaleia, who wasn't afraid of getting hurt or letting someone into her life. Although that unguarded moment might have had something to do with kissing someone entirely unsuitable.

Perhaps she did need to have more fun and kiss handsome boys if she was ever to get over the past. Enzo Capelli might just be the way to do it.

CHAPTER FIVE

IF IT WEREN'T for the fact he was expected at this party, Enzo would be tempted to haul anchor and sail off on his next adventure. He'd made a stupid, stupid mistake in kissing Thaleia. She wasn't just some party girl out for a good time who'd forget him as soon as he'd forget her. Thaleia was Alex's little sister, for goodness' sake. He'd put the 'No sisters' pact in serious jeopardy, and likely ruined any chance of ever being part of his best friend's life again. That was if Thaleia told him. Enzo had to hold onto that small hope that their distant relationship these days wouldn't necessitate her sharing that particular piece of information with her brother.

The book he'd been pretending to read for the past hour slid to the floor from his knee. He'd holed himself up in the yacht for a couple of days. The only people he'd interacted with were the crew, who'd made sure he was fed and not lounging around in bed, wallowing in his own lack of judgement. They were almost like family, even if he did have to pay them. Constantly checking in on him, and coaxing him out into the fresh air.

He had no defence for his actions. Only that he'd got caught up in the moment. Forgotten who she was, and what they were doing. Acting in the moment when desire overtook common sense. Now it was down to her to decide if she was going to continue working for him, or attend the party as his plus one. Thanks to Thaleia Galatis, it would seem he'd developed a conscience, as well as a penchant for spiky, beautiful Greek jewellers.

His phone rang in his pocket and he was about to reject the call when he saw who it was calling.

'Thaleia. Hi.'

'I, er, just wanted to say thanks for the beautiful bouquet you sent. There really wasn't any need.' She sounded a little nervous, and no wonder when a man she hardly knew, a customer, had kissed her when she'd been trying to help him. It didn't matter that she'd responded, kissed him back with just as much conviction. He should never have done it. Especially knowing her opinion of him and that he was probably the last man in the world she'd considered kissing up until then.

He was used to being the leader of the pack and everyone more than happy to go along with him. It had been a long time since he'd had to exercise any impulse control, but he was going to have to learn, and fast, if Thaleia let him back into her life.

'I just wanted to apologise. Again.' He'd waited a couple of days then sent a huge bouquet of flowers with one word on the card. *Sorry.* In the hope she would forgive him and still go to this party.

'Really. There's no need. As you said, it was probably the shock impairing your judgement, and the sun affecting mine. It's best forgotten.'

'Thank you.' He thought better of saying anything else on the subject and let it drop as she suggested.

'The reason I was calling was because I've finished the necklace. I thought you might like to see it.'

'Yes. Of course. You must have been working overtime to get it finished so soon.'

'You could say that.' Her laugh made him wonder if she'd been trying to keep herself busy since that kiss too. Although her time appeared to have been more productive than his.

'Would you like me to send a boat for you? Or should I come to you?' This time he wasn't going to impose himself on her. He'd accepted the fact he'd been taking that control away from her by making those decisions on her behalf. By letting her take that control back he hoped she would see that he had only good intentions.

'If it's not too late I was thinking you could come here. You also promised to make me dinner at some point…'

Her request was surprising in more ways than one. Up until this phone call he'd imagined she'd never want to even see him again. Perhaps this was her way of saying all was forgiven. If she was willing to let him into her house again it was a sign she didn't see him as any kind of threat. He simply had to make sure it never happened again.

'I'm happy to bring supplies over, if that's what you want? I'm sure the chef will be only too glad of a night off.' It was an olive branch, one he was happy to take.

'So will I. That's settled, then. Be at mine for seven thirty and I'll have a pinny waiting for you.' Enzo could hear the smile in her voice now. She sounded more relaxed, the awkward tension between them suddenly dissipating, and relief flooded his body too.

'I will see you then.' When Enzo ended the call he had a smile on his face. A transformation from the frown that had been ever present since he'd messed up and kissed Thaleia.

This was his second chance. Thaleia was simply doing a job for him. They had made an agreement to be each other's dates with no strings attached. She was Alex's little sister. There was absolutely no excuse for him to go kissing her again.

Thaleia wiped down her already clean dining table, and adjusted the cutlery she'd laid out earlier. Since coming off the phone to Enzo she hadn't been able to settle. During working hours she'd managed to keep herself busy. Thankfully, there had been an influx of tourists these past few days, which had not only boosted her coffers but called for her to make more stock for the shop.

When she finished the pendant necklace for Enzo, she knew she had to contact him again. That was when she made the decision to face things head-on. One kiss didn't have to derail everything when it meant nothing. He probably kissed a dozen women a day.

OK, that might have been an exaggeration, but she doubted he was losing sleep over kissing her. It was entirely her fault that she was replaying the moment in her head more than the one when she found out her groom wasn't coming to their wedding.

Now, when Enzo was going to be here any minute, she didn't know what to do with herself.

It wasn't a date, not even a business meeting, so there was no reason she should be so jittery.

Yet when the doorbell sounded announcing his presence, it still made her jump. Made her pulse quicken and her tummy flip.

She took a deep breath, steadied herself and walked over to the door. 'Enzo. Thank you for coming.'

He peered out from behind the large bag of groceries he was carrying. 'Well, you didn't give me much of a choice, did you? Demanding I come and cook you dinner…'

He was grinning as he made his way into her home and into the kitchen. Thaleia wondered if he ever worried at all, took anything seriously, or simply went through life laughing and joking. She wondered what it was to be that carefree. Enzo Capelli would likely always be the heart-breaker, not the heartbroken.

'I know. I'm such a diva.' She handed him an apron and managed to suppress a giggle as he tied the frilly-edged garment around his waist.

'You know, this is a complete change of situation for me,' he said, his head cocked to one side. 'Usually I'm the one giving instructions and having people do my bidding.'

'Then this will be a learning experience for you, Enzo.' Thaleia took a seat in the kitchen, watching him unload the groceries.

'I don't think it's something either of us should get too used to.'

She knew he was referring to the fact he was waiting on her tonight, instead of his staff catering to his every whim, but she knew it worked on other levels too. They shouldn't get accustomed to one another's company when he would be on the move again soon.

'So what are we having?' Thaleia leaned her elbow on the counter, watching as the ingredients tumbled out of his bag.

'Pizza.'

'You're kidding me.'

'What's wrong with pizza?' He looked visibly upset when she queried his menu choice, but she had to admit she was a little underwhelmed.

'When an Italian offers to cook there are certain things expected. Like fresh homemade pasta, and white-wine sauces. Not something I can pull out of the freezer and cook in twelve minutes.'

Enzo clutched his chest. 'You wound me. This isn't some generic store-bought pizza. It's authentic Italian pizza like my mamma used to make.'

'I apologise. I'll hold my judgement until after a taste test.' Thaleia immediately felt contrite for slighting his culinary skills and his heritage as he lifted out a covered glass bowl with a ball of dough inside.

'It was the first thing my mother taught me how to make. She was more at home in the kitchen than anywhere else. I have all of her recipes tucked away up here.' He tapped a finger at his temple.

'You must have been close.' Thaleia would be surprised if her mother even knew where the kitchen was, never mind getting her hands dirty, or teaching her daughter how to cook.

He nodded. A solemnity enveloping him at the mere mention. 'I was lucky. I had the most amazing parents. Mother provided the love and comfort, and Father was always there with his words of wisdom, or anything else we might need from him.'

Thaleia envied the close bond Enzo seemed to have had with his parents, but acknowledged that had also come at a price. She realised how devastated he must've been by their deaths. Losing that love and support so suddenly would have been a terrible shock for someone so young.

'I'm so sorry that you lost them.' She didn't know what else to say and Enzo gave her a sad smile in response.

'Well, I'm glad I'm getting to share something of their legacy with you tonight.' It was a touching sentiment, and Thaleia could see now why a simple pizza meant so much more. She was privileged that he felt comfortable enough with her to share the memory along with his cooking.

'I should take some lessons myself.' Her own cooking talents were limited. A privileged lifestyle wasn't conducive to learning such basic life skills when people were paid to do it. Though since moving to the island she'd had to learn how to use the oven more when lifting the phone to order food wasn't really an option. The closest she came to that was Agathi calling with her cart full of goodies.

'I prepped a few things so we didn't have to wait two hours for the dough to rise. I haven't done this for a long time. I forgot how therapeutic it was.' Enzo was kneading the dough now, looking every inch the expert.

'What do you have to worry about? How deep your tan is? If there is enough champagne on board your yacht to last the week?' Thaleia attempted some levity to lighten the mood.

When he gave a heavy sigh in response, instead of a witty retort, or even a scowl, she could have kicked herself for seeming insensitive. 'I wish it were as simple as that. That all my problems could be solved with some sunbathing and a phone call to the nearest bar.'

Thaleia seemed to be putting her foot in it quite a bit, and she put it down to nerves. In trying to get things between them on a more platonic basis, she'd managed to insult and upset him instead.

'Sorry. I thought I was being funny. I didn't realise you had other things going on.'

Another wobbly smile that made her heart ache for him. It was clear there was something eating away at him, but, credit to him, he'd been doing a stand-up job of hiding whatever it was up until now.

'I just wish Bea and I were closer. It's my own fault, but I do miss having family around.'

'And there's no hope of a reconciliation?' She knew how it felt to be distanced from family. Although it had been her choice to have some space away from her parents, she hadn't been given any say in losing Alex. She'd imagined that he'd come back home after university, but she'd lost him to Enzo, then to Georgios. She missed him and, given half a chance, she'd like to spend time with both her brother and her nephew. To really feel like part of a proper family.

'It's not that we even had a real falling-out. Perhaps if we had, it might be easier to send a bunch of flowers with an apology note.' This time he gave her a proper smile. 'We've just never been close. Actually, that's a lie. We were when she was very small. I was her big brother and it's fair to say she idolised me. I just wish

I'd deserved it. When our parents died, I was responsible for her, but we were both grieving, and dealing with the huge upheaval in our lives. I thought it was better for her to go to boarding school while I was at university. At least there, she'd have people around her. Structure I didn't think I was capable of providing. Now though, I don't think I did enough. Bea was only eight years old. She'd lost her parents, moved to a new country, and her big brother had gone off to university. I should have been there for her more.'

It was clear to Thaleia that he was battling his conscience over the way things had played out, regardless that he'd been grieving too.

'Has your sister ever said she was unhappy? Was she upset whenever you visited her?'

Enzo paused, obviously thinking it over before answering. 'No. I don't think so. If she had, I would definitely have done something about it.'

'You know, it's entirely possible you're blaming yourself needlessly. You were both grieving in incredibly difficult circumstances, losing everything you'd ever known. I'm sure you did what you thought was best at the time.'

'I guess…' Enzo was frowning, as though suddenly seeing his past in a new light.

'Have you and Beatrice ever had a proper talk about what happened, or how you felt at the time?'

'No.'

'Did Bea ever lay blame at your feet for her being unhappy?'

'No. I accepted responsibility myself.'

'Unnecessarily, in my opinion. And you say there was no big falling-out?'

'No. We just kind of drifted apart. She trained as a teacher, and I took to the high seas.'

'Then I don't think it's too late to rescue your relationship. If you reached out to her and talked the way we are doing now, I'm sure you could sort things out.' Thaleia would be willing to put the past behind her and Alex if she got another chance to be a sister and an aunt. As it was, the emotional distance between them made it impossible. Their parents had driven Alex away from the home, and, as a result, had put a wedge between the siblings. A shame when he'd been her sanctuary growing up. Keeping her away from their parents' arguments, and providing a safe space for her. Making her feel loved.

The physical distance when he'd been at university, as well as the age gap, meant they'd found it hard to connect on any real meaningful level. Something she would be willing to work on if it meant she could have him and Georgios in her life. She missed the big brother who'd looked after her, but she supposed his son needed him more.

'Perhaps. I'm not sure how she feels about me at all. If she even cares.' It was clear Enzo was determined to think the worst of himself, barely entertaining the idea that Bea would simply love him for who he was. Hopefully, Thaleia was giving him something to think about and he might reconsider his stance in the future.

'I'm sure she does. You're her brother, her only family. I'm sure if she thought you were willing to repair your relationship, she'd make the effort too.' Thaleia mulled over what she was saying for a moment before adding, 'It's probably about time I took my own advice too. I keep thinking about how much I'm missing Alex but I haven't actually told him that.'

'You should. I know for a fact he's very fond of you. He used to talk a lot about you, and I know he missed you when we were at university together. There was an old photograph he had of the two of you he kept in his wallet. I think you were on the beach.'

'That was our favourite place to be.' It really touched her to hear that. In her mind Alex had simply gone away and forgotten about her. Too busy having fun to give a second thought to the little sister he'd left at home. Much like Enzo and his sister, it was possible they'd simply got too involved in their own lives to pay attention to their relationship.

Enzo separated his dough into two mounds. 'Come on. It sounds as though you need some therapy too.'

Thaleia got up off her seat and washed her hands before she came to join him. 'I thought you were supposed to be cooking for me.'

'Call it a lesson in Italian cooking instead. A new life skill you can carry forward.' He took some flour and dusted it over her hands, the unexpected contact temporarily making her forget this was supposed to be a platonic night in together. His touch electrifying and tender all at the same time. It was difficult not to think about what that touch might be like in an entirely different setting. Especially after that sizzling kiss.

'You're too kind.' She fell back on sarcasm as her defence mechanism against those feelings he was capable of stirring up inside her. For some reason Thaleia had imagined that moving here in the middle of nowhere would somehow remove those urges towards the opposite sex, so she'd never have to worry about having her heart broken again. Mr Capelli was proving that wasn't the case. A change in location and lifestyle hadn't made her any less of a hot-blooded woman.

'Just stretch out the dough into a circle. That's it. A little olive oil, then we're going to spoon some tomato sauce over that I made earlier.'

Enzo spread the sauce over his dough before handing it over to Thaleia.

'I'm hoping it's the mozzarella next. It's making me hungry looking at it.'

Enzo sliced up the mozzarella and passed over a generous portion for Thaleia to cover her base. 'Basil next, and a little more olive oil.'

Between them they managed to create two delicious-looking pizzas, which he popped into the pre-heated oven. 'It won't take too long. I think we've got time to enjoy a nice glass of white wine while we wait.'

He produced a chilled bottle of wine from a cooler in his bag of tricks.

'I swear you must have your own vineyard somewhere.' Thaleia produced two glasses, having decided it was safe enough to indulge now that her working day was over.

'Not yet, but I'm considering it.'

'Really?'

'I have been in touch with a few people recently. It's an interest I'm currently pursuing.'

'That sounds as though it might require you to come ashore a bit more often.' The thought wasn't as abhorrent to Thaleia as she'd thought after their first meeting.

'I haven't made a decision yet, but I am beginning to think there's maybe more to life than floating around the world drinking champagne.'

'You think?' Thaleia raised an eyebrow. To find out there was more and more to the man behind the reputation wasn't helping her keep her emotions in check. Not when he'd already made it clear in talking about his sister that he did care about more than himself. And he was here, showing her how to make pizza and finding common ground over their estranged siblings. Enzo Capelli was becoming three-dimensional. No longer a caricature of a man, but a living, breathing human being with emotions and problems just like everyone else. She might even say he was 4D. So much more complex than she'd given him credit for.

'Believe it or not, Thaleia, even playboys have another side to them.' He held her under his intense gaze, sending shivers up and down the back of her neck.

'I'm beginning to see that,' she said, sipping her wine, and trying not to let him see how that version of him was beginning to affect her. That the reasons she had for not getting close to him were gradually slipping away.

Not only was he beginning to rethink his lifestyle, but he was talking about setting down roots. Literally. Making it harder for her to not like him as much as she did. Of course, it didn't matter how much she liked him, because she couldn't allow anything to happen between them anyway. One broken heart in a lifetime was plenty.

The timer on the oven beeped and jolted them back out of the moment.

Enzo removed both pizzas and set them onto the plates before expertly slicing them up. 'It's difficult to tell whose was whose.'

Thaleia laughed as he presented her with the mozzarella-heavy dish she'd prepared, compared to the beautifully aesthetic version that could have come straight from an Italian pizzeria.

She lifted her knife and fork, but before she could cut into her food, Enzo's hand covered hers.

'What are you doing?'

'I was trying to eat my dinner.' Thaleia's brow was knotted into a frown. She hadn't figured him as religious but perhaps he wanted to say grace before they tucked in.

'Yes, but this is a Capelli family tradition I want you to be a part of too—no cutlery.' Enzo picked up a slice of her pizza, almost folding it in half as he lifted it towards her mouth.

Thaleia bit into the piping-hot pizza, a string of cheese stretching between them.

'There's no elegant way of eating it like that, is there?' she said once she'd swallowed it down.

'But it tastes good, yes? I have good memories of us all sitting around the table eating like this. Laughing and enjoying just being together.' Enzo shared another precious moment with her before tucking into his own pizza and letting her feed herself the rest of her slice.

The rest of the pizza didn't taste quite as good without being hand-fed by a gorgeous Italian, but she finished another couple of slices nonetheless. Enzo, on the other hand, cleared his plate with gusto.

'I couldn't eat another bite.' Thaleia pushed her plate aside, though she'd enjoyed the meal, and the company.

'You can always have it tomorrow. Are you saving that bit of basil between your teeth too?'

'Oh.' Thaleia clamped her mouth shut at once, embarrassed at the thought, just as Enzo reached out. It resulted in her closing her lips around Enzo's thumb, making things even more humiliating.

Except he took his time pulling away, trailing his thumb tenderly over her bottom lip. Looking at her with undisguised hunger, and causing her own body to respond accordingly. Waiting and wanting him to make the next move.

The moment was crackling with sexual tension, her body taut with need and longing, but Thaleia couldn't take that next step. She had the feeling he was waiting for her to give him consent to repeat their last mistake, but old wounds prevented her from giving into temptation. Now that they'd come to know each other better, a kiss felt more dangerous than it had that day they'd been to the beach. Enzo was no longer just a playboy. He was a grieving son, a lonely brother to Bea, and a man willing to come and show her how he used to make pizza with his mother. There were emotional layers to him she hadn't realised existed and that could prove detrimental to her already fragile heart.

If she kissed him again, this time it might lead to something more, and then what? She was leaving herself vulnerable to a man who hadn't yet decided what he wanted to be when he grew up. Who couldn't even maintain a relationship with the only family member he had left. It wasn't the making of an ideal relationship and she needed some sort of stability in a partner if she was ever going to venture out of singledom again.

She was relieved, if disappointed, when Enzo sat back in his chair, creating a void between them. 'I should probably get back before it gets much later.'

'Oh, I never got to show you the finished necklace.' It occurred to Thaleia that they'd both completely forgotten the reason he'd come to her place. She didn't know what that said other than it had proved a good excuse for them to spend the evening together.

'Of course. If you want to get it ready for me to take, I'll get cleaned up here, ready to go.' Enzo was making it clear this was the end of the evening, and Thaleia decided it was probably for the best. The longer they spent together, the more dangerously close they came to crossing that line again.

She hurried into the shop and, after a last-minute polish, she arranged the necklace in a suitably luxurious silk-lined, blue-velvet presentation case. When she returned to her part of the house, the kitchen was spotless and Enzo looked ready to leave.

Thaleia was suddenly nervous about showing him the piece. Worried it wasn't up to the standards he'd hoped for or expected. That she'd let him down in some way, even though she'd been proud of her work up until this very moment. Goodness knew how her nerves were going to hold out when the recipient actually received her gift.

She opened the case and held her breath, waiting to see his genuine reaction, not the one he wanted her to see.

'It's amazing, Thaleia. Thank you.' His beaming grin managed to relax every muscle in her tense body.

'Do you think Irida will like it?' She hated to sound so needy for praise, but there was a lot riding on this influential woman appreciating her gift enough to wear it.

'I'm sure she'll love it.' Enzo leaned in and gave her a quick peck on the cheek, but the moment they made contact, it felt as though they'd triggered something.

He paused, as though he was debating what to do next. His breath hot on her cheek, her body tensed with anticipation, breath caught somewhere in her throat as she waited. A second seemed an eternity before he gave into whatever had been holding him back and kissed her on the lips. A kiss so soft she might have dreamed it had happened at all except for the longing it had awoken in her for more. Then Enzo turned his head away, denying her more.

'Goodnight, Thaleia.' His voice was thick with desire, but he was already walking towards the door.

Perhaps he wasn't as reckless as he led people to believe after all. Although, the more time she spent with him, the more Thaleia was beginning to believe that wild side was rubbing off on her. It was easy to see why her brother had been so influenced by such a charismatic, spontaneous character when Enzo made her want to step out of her comfort zone and take a risk every now and then. Even if it was just kissing someone she knew she shouldn't.

CHAPTER SIX

'ENZO? I WASN'T expecting you until the party.' Irida Angelopoulos kissed him on both cheeks before inviting him inside her palatial home.

'Sorry for the unannounced visit.'

'Is something wrong?' She directed him to the floral chaise longue while she took a seat opposite.

'Not at all. I just thought I'd bring your birthday gift over early. I know you'll be busy at the party and, well, I thought I'd add a more personal touch than simply being added to the pile on the night.' He handed over the gift-wrapped necklace and waited with bated breath.

'How lovely. Let me get you a drink and we can celebrate properly.' Irida called for her assistant who was soon hurrying off to do her bidding.

Enzo couldn't help but wonder what Thaleia would make of this setting. Irida was bedecked in jewels and an almost luminous pink kaftan paired with very tight, unflattering leggings with a tropical leaf motif. An outfit that likely cost more than the average national wage, but didn't impress him as much as Thaleia's simple sundress she'd worn that day on the beach.

It occurred to him that she could be wearing a sack and he'd still think she was the most beautiful being in creation. Kissing her again had been inevitable, he supposed, once he'd known how she felt in his arms, and tasted on his lips. That didn't mean it had been a good idea. Those reasons he'd tried to hold onto to prevent him making the same mistake were still there, even if he had slipped up again.

He liked her too much, had too much respect for her to bed her and leave her. That was who Enzo Capelli was. He wasn't the settling-down, family man she needed and he didn't want to hurt her. However, they'd agreed to be one another's dates for these social events and he didn't want to let anyone down. Either Thaleia or Irida. He figured the only way to ensure that could still happen was to stay out of Thaleia's way until then. Coming here in advance of the party seemed a good excuse to keep busy. He also hoped he could talk his friend into wearing Thaleia's necklace so she might benefit from the publicity.

He watched as Irida tore off the curled ribbons and paper one of his stewards had wrapped his gift in, tossing it onto the floor with glee. Perfectly manicured neon-pink acrylic nails traced the curve of the sapphire and diamond wave Thaleia had created. He understood how nervous she must have been when she'd given it to him for his approval because he felt the same way now. Waiting, and watching, hoping that the birthday girl liked it.

'It's beautiful, Enzo. Thank you.' Her enhanced plump lips smiled at him.

'I had it made specially for you by a friend of mine. She says it's a symbol of the island that you can keep with you wherever you may be.' Special to him too because he knew how much love and effort Thaleia had put into creating the piece for him. He'd almost been tempted to keep it for himself but it would have been a shame if no one else got to see her work.

'It's stunning.' She looked at the necklace, then at Enzo. 'Now tell me why you're really here.'

At that moment, the member of staff came bustling back in with two glasses of what looked like ready-prepared cocktails. Margaritas, he suspected, since they were known to be a favourite of Irida's. He wasn't a huge fan but he wanted to be a welcome guest, and had come to ask a favour, so he accepted the glass gratefully.

He sipped the drink, getting that hit of salt

around the rim first, making him wince. 'I told you—to bring you your gift.'

Irida cocked her head to one side and managed to lift an eyebrow despite her remarkably smooth forehead. 'Enzo, usually you rock up at these things late, if at all, with a couple of attractive young women on your arm. Paying no heed to anyone else, making us feel as though we're lucky you even showed your face. So I'll ask again, what is it you really want?'

That mirror being held up to his face wasn't a flattering one. Was that really how he appeared to people? Self-obsessed, self-absorbed, and flaky? It was no wonder Thaleia hadn't wanted to know him at first. This version of him his friend seemed to know wasn't the same man he was with Thaleia. Perhaps that was because he wasn't playing a part with her. He wasn't the playboy millionaire he projected to the rest of the world because she didn't need him to be.

They'd had more fun doing the simple things in life like going to the beach and making pizza, things that made him feel as though he could have been any other man in the world. There was no need for throwing money around and being the life and soul of the party because she wasn't impressed by that. Enzo had to admit it was nice being able to turn it all off when he was with her. Sometimes it was exhausting, and he was happier when it was just the two of them. Perhaps he didn't need to be surrounded by pandering strangers if he had the right person next to him.

It was a shame that couldn't possibly be Thaleia when he'd made a pact with her brother to keep away from her. Something he was already in breach of, and taking it any further could damage relations with the entire Galatis family.

'OK, you got me.' He turned on the full-beam smile, figuring he had to deploy playboy Enzo on this occasion if he was to get his friend's co-operation. 'The necklace was made for me by Thaleia Galatis.'

It wasn't long before the name rang a bell with his friend. 'That poor girl who was jilted at the altar?'

Thaleia would hate that was how she was recognised now. It was no wonder she'd distanced herself from her old life, trying to make a new one for herself if she was ever to get away from that stigma. Regardless that she'd been the victim and didn't deserve to drag around with her that burden implying that she was a failure in some way.

'Yes. Her brother, Alexandros, is a friend of mine. She's running her own business now and I hoped you might wear her work at the party to give her a little boost.'

'Of course. I probably would have worn it anyway. It's beautiful.'

Enzo was relieved he wasn't asking too much, and hopefully hadn't crossed the line of friendship. Real friends were hard to come by for a man like him, and apparently easily lost.

'Thank you. It will mean a lot to Thaleia.'

'Is she coming with you to the party?'

'Yes, I thought it would be good exposure for her. A chance to network.'

'She means a lot to you.' Irida peered at him over the rim of her glass.

'I told you, her brother's a friend.'

'Uh-huh.' She set her drink down on the glass table in front of her, studying Enzo so carefully he felt like a bug under a microscope.

'Alex and I went to university together. Thaleia works on the island so I thought your birthday gift gave me the perfect opportunity to connect with her.' His mouth was dry, but his bitter drink did nothing to sate him. This was beginning to feel like some sort of therapy session, or a confessional. Either way, he suspected he was being asked to examine himself more closely and the idea terrified him. He'd been running away from real life his whole adult life and he didn't want to face the consequences of that head-on. It meant dealing with emotions. Ones that had been locked away, and new ones that were beginning to surface.

He had a feeling his playboy days were coming to an end and he wasn't sure where that left him. Possibly completely on his own.

'You could have sent this with a note. Asked for a separate invitation for Thaleia to attend the party, leaving you free to bring one of your usual…dates. I think you like this girl. You're just too afraid to admit it and ruin your reputation.' The sly smile was set on her face as though she'd discovered some salacious new piece of gossip.

Enzo had no choice but to come clean in the hope of stemming any more damage to Thaleia's reputation. He certainly didn't want anything to reach Alex's ears. All he could do was either introduce her as his friend or keep her entirely at a distance. He supposed he should let her make the call before she scolded him for making decisions on her behalf again.

'I like her, yes, but we're just friends. That's all we can be. I'm just trying to do her a favour.' All of which was true. Irida didn't need to know the rest.

She studied him a bit longer before sighing and draining the rest of her drink. 'Well, she'd be lucky to have you. I know you have a reputation with the ladies that isn't the greatest, but you have a good heart. One you wouldn't give away easily, so be careful.'

He appreciated the warning but coming here was already a step away from Thaleia. Once his obligation to her was over he'd be leaving and she'd soon be a distant memory.

At least, in theory. He knew the reality was going to be very different, and difficult.

'Are you sure you're OK going in together?' Enzo asked as they stepped out of the limo he'd rented for the evening. He looked so handsome. Thaleia realised she was thinking that a lot these days, along with the fact that she was starting to really like him.

Not that anything could come of it. A couple of kisses and they'd had to spend days apart to make sure nothing more happened. Enzo had even rung to check she wanted to attend this party with him at all, with some excuse about people reading more into it than she'd be happy with. She didn't care. Thaleia was done with hiding away. Her business was more important to her than what people thought.

Besides, this was the first time she'd ventured out in public since her non-wedding and she needed someone to hold her hand through it.

'Definitely. I need some emotional support.'

Right on cue, Enzo put his hand at the small

of her back and guided her past everyone gathering at the front of the mansion. Reminding her that he was there for her, hopefully for the rest of the evening.

Although she was used to these kinds of soirées, her skin was clammy and her heart was racing as they made their way inside. It had been a while since she'd been in any sort of a crowd, and the noise, the sight of so many people in one space, was almost overwhelming.

'Are you OK?' Enzo whispered into her ear, sending goosebumps all over her skin. He'd obviously sensed her unease, the sudden tension in her body and the hesitation to walk further into the throng.

'It's just…a lot.' As well as the well-dressed guests, there were living statues walking around with trays of food and drinks. People made up to look like stone carvings adorned in togas and laurel wreaths. Some dressed as ancient Greek gods.

Then there was the group in the foyer wearing traditional costume and playing rousing tunes as people entered the house. No doubt once sufficient alcohol had been taken there would be dancing as well by the attendees.

'I know, but that's Irida for you. She's a lot too.' Enzo nodded towards the grand staircase, where the woman of the hour made her appearance.

The band played her arrival, stopping everyone in their tracks.

Thaleia had seen her at various functions in the past and she was always a striking figure, but here, completely uninhibited, she was a sight to behold. 'I'm suddenly feeling very underdressed.'

'Nonsense. You're the most stunning woman here.' Enzo's compliment, which may have been simply to put her at ease, nonetheless gave her a warm glow inside.

Irida was wearing a white silk halter-neck dress edged in silver. Her pneumatic breasts barely covered by the draped fabric. On her head she wore a diamond and sapphire tiara on a very elaborate copper-coloured wig, ringlets falling around her bare shoulders. To top the Greek goddess look, a giant pair of wings sprouted from her back. Most noticeable to Thaleia, though, was the necklace she had made, proudly dangling around the woman's bare neck.

'She's wearing my necklace.' Thaleia was talking to herself in disbelief, as much as to Enzo.

'Of course. I told you she loved it. Why don't I introduce you?' Enzo was guiding Thaleia towards the host before she had time to properly compose herself.

'Ah, Enzo. So glad you came, and, Thaleia,

it's so nice to see you.' Irida kissed them on both cheeks, the feathers from her wings tickling Thaleia's nose in the process.

'Happy birthday, and, may I say, you look amazing.' Thaleia took a step back to take in the full effect of the outfit again.

'You may.' Irida laughed as she tossed her fake red ringlets over her shoulder.

'Thank you for wearing the necklace. It looks good on you. You decided to accessorise, I see?' Enzo pointed towards the tiara perched perilously atop her luscious locks.

'Always. The necklace was perfect, my dear, but I wanted to add more impact. I hope you're not offended.' She took Thaleia's hand so earnestly, it was impossible to be upset.

'Not at all. It all works perfectly together.' Given how much Enzo had paid for the necklace, Thaleia could only imagine the price of the tiara. She wondered if it was a family heirloom that had been retrieved from a safety-deposit box for the occasion, or if it had been an impulse buy. Either option was possible with someone like Irida, whose wealthy family went back generations, but she was also noted for her impulsive, extravagant spending.

'I'll be happy to pass on your details to anyone who shows an interest, Thaleia, dear. Now, if you don't mind, I must mingle. Go, enjoy yourselves.' Although it was Irida who moved away, it felt very much as though she was dismissing them. She was a charismatic, enigmatic woman, and Thaleia loved her already. It was little wonder her parents were always keen to have Irida attend any of their functions. She held court like a queen, and people naturally gravitated towards her, evident by the number swarming around her and how long it took her to simply walk across the foyer.

'I think that's this mission accomplished.' Enzo grabbed two glasses of champagne from a passing statue and handed one to Thaleia so they could raise a toast.

'Just one more to go.' She couldn't say she was particularly looking forward to that one. She didn't have a goal there other than to survive the evening relatively unscathed.

CHAPTER SEVEN

ENZO COULD SEE Thaleia relax once they'd spoken to Irida, and the birthday girl seemed happy too. He could see her chatting animatedly to a crowd of wide-eyed young women, touching her necklace, then pointing over at Thaleia.

'Looks like she might be drumming up some business for you,' he told her.

'I should have brought business cards with me. I just thought it might seem a bit gauche to be touting for business at someone's birthday party.' She was fretting again, already imagining she'd failed in some way. It was a different side to her from the one he was used to. On their own, she was a firecracker, standing her ground at any cost. Here in public she seemed nervous, unsure of herself, when there was no need to be. Enzo supposed it was down to her ex. Being publicly rejected, humiliated in front of friends and family, not to mention the rich families who were no doubt in attendance too, was bound to have had an effect on her self-esteem. He hoped tonight would help give her a confidence boost again.

'It'll be fine. Irida will pass on your name and anyone who wants to will find some way of getting in touch. Stop worrying and just enjoy the party as we were instructed.' He held out his arm for Thaleia to take and escorted her outside to the vast grounds at the back of the house where most of the party appeared to be taking place.

There was a DJ playing loud thumping music, coloured lights and lasers dancing in time to the beat. Casting purple and vivid green rays across the assembled guests.

'There's a cocktail bar. Can we get one? I think it'll help me wind down a little.' Thaleia pointed towards the makeshift tiki bar that had been set up poolside serving bright drinks garnished with coloured umbrellas and sliced fruit.

'Of course. I'm not sure what the theme is supposed to be here exactly, with a traditional Greek group and costumes inside, and a rave out here.' It was two contrasting areas, with no apparent common ground. Although that was Irida all over. She didn't care what anyone thought of her, her dress or her lifestyle. With no family responsibilities, she simply did as she pleased. Enzo could relate to a point. As Thaleia had pointed out, at some stage all the partying and trying to recapture youth through young guests would begin to look a little tragic.

Goodness knew he didn't want to reach his sixties dressing like a Greek god, with virtual strangers pandering to him, because he'd been too self-absorbed to consider a family. Or pushed the only one he had away.

'Perhaps she's simply trying to cater for everybody. Make sure everyone is happy,' Thaleia suggested.

Enzo knew he was guilty of doing that too. Going all out to ensure everyone had a good time so it reflected well on him. Watching from the outside, he was beginning to see just how lonely that life was. He wondered if Irida, given the chance to live her life over again, would rather have settled down with a soulmate and filled her house with children instead of strangers.

Once upon a time, he might have considered that himself. Hoping to replicate the joyful home he'd had with his parents and Beatrice. When he'd been happy. But losing everything had made him wary of getting close to anyone in case he lost them too. Messing up the relationship with Beatrice, not being what she'd needed, only emphasised that notion that he was better off alone. Even now, he was losing his best friend because he couldn't relate to where Alex was in life. A father. A role Enzo could never see himself in.

Perhaps if his parents had still been around he might have taken the leap and committed to a relationship instead of becoming someone they would never recognise. A rudderless man trying to drown out feelings of grief and guilt with parties and women.

He glanced at Thaleia as the bartender dressed in neon clothes handed her a cocktail. A bowl-shaped glass containing a bright orange liquid with some sort of paper parrot decoration perched on the edge. She looked so happy.

Her eyes were sparkling. Full pink lips smiling broadly at him. She was beautiful and content. He couldn't remember the last time he'd felt like that. All she'd wanted was a husband who loved her. It didn't seem a lot to expect, yet he could relate in some way to the man who'd left her at the altar. A lifetime commitment to another person was simply too much to expect from some people. From him.

Yet, lately, he'd found himself searching for ways to make Thaleia happy. The meals together, getting his friend to promote her work, he'd got more satisfaction from watching her reaction to these things than his own. Surely that was a sign that he was changing? Maturing. Showing that he wasn't as selfish as he'd once been. When he'd done everything to make himself feel good so he never had time to dwell on the bad things that had happened to him.

He wished he could show Beatrice he'd changed. Make amends with her too by making room in his life for her. Though he had a feeling it would take more than a party at someone else's place to salvage that relationship.

'Are you enjoying that?' he asked with a smile as the liquid in Thaleia's glass started disappearing.

'Yes. It's very refreshing. Would you like some?'

'No, thanks. I'll stick to the champagne. Why don't we go and take a seat by the pool?' They took their drinks, and Enzo, having seen some of the more exuberant dancers bustling into people, guided her towards a quieter area.

'I would have thought you'd be in the middle of all of this. Chugging back alcohol and strutting your stuff on the dance floor,' Thaleia teased, nodding towards the young partygoers who seemed to be here to have the best time ever.

'Not tonight. I'm off duty.' For once, Enzo was simply interested in getting away as soon as possible. Before he got to that stage. Party-boy Enzo was not going to impress Thaleia, and that would spoil everything he'd been working towards. Because he wanted her to like him. He didn't know why it was important other than the fact he was himself around her. And having her like the 'real' Enzo made him think that there was still hope for him not to end up like their exuberant, but possibly lonely, host.

'You make it sound like a job.'

'I suppose, when I look at it, it is. All the planning and preparing. Hosting. Not to mention keeping up the energy levels. It's only just occurring to me that it's a lot of work being an international playboy.' He was only partly joking. Analysing everything about his life these past few days was making him question what he was doing, and why. Of course, it had been fun along the way, but it was beginning to become more of a chore. Perhaps even a hindrance to the person he wanted to be. That was a man worthy of Thaleia and his sister. Even if he couldn't be with either of them.

'Maybe you should start a business.' Thaleia shrugged as though it were as easy as having the thought. Although, he supposed, with his money and connections, it probably was.

'You seem determined to have me gainfully employed, despite my extensive business success.'

'By your own admission, Enzo, you inherited that business, and other people run it for you. I'm not saying that's a bad thing, except you don't seem particularly happy or content at present. It's not healthy to lead the lifestyle you have. I just think perhaps an outside interest would be good for you.'

'Do you need a business partner?' He gave a bitter laugh, because she had him pinned. She could see beyond the bravado and the flirty façade to see that he needed something more in his life. He was simply afraid of the responsibility and duty that would come with any commitment. Family, business or otherwise. And the possibility that it would all come crashing down around him. Devastating him all over again.

There was that roll of her eyes at him again that made him genuinely laugh. 'You need to actively participate in something. Get off that yacht and onto dry land. Back to reality.'

'That's coming from someone who's been hiding away on an island for months…' He took a swig of champagne, wishing it were something stronger if he was going to be confronted by the waste his life had become.

It was one thing figuring it out for himself, but quite another having Thaleia point it out to him. Making him go into defensive mode rather than admit to her his life was lacking something. Because that meant confessing he'd realised it was her he'd be missing in his life once he moved on from the island.

Instead of taking offence, getting upset or throwing insults at him, Thaleia simply said, 'Touché.'

They sat for a few moments in silence, sipping their drinks, and respectively mulling over their existence, he supposed. It wasn't the night he'd planned, or the atmosphere he usually cultivated at such an event. Although he had no intention of reverting back to type, the least he could do was show her a good time.

He set his drink down, got up, took Thaleia's glass from her and set it down too.

'What are you doing?' she spluttered as he took her hand and helped her out of her seat.

'We didn't come here to get maudlin and miserable. This is supposed to be a party. A celebration.' Enzo led her back towards the makeshift dance floor on the patio where revellers had gathered in front of the DJ to boogie.

'Enzo…' The wariness was there in her tone, as well as in her eyes. That hesitation in trusting him, and no wonder with his reputation.

However, in that moment, Enzo realised he never wanted to do anything that would hurt her. She'd been hurt once too often and deserved only the best. In the long term, he knew, that wasn't him, but hopefully, for a short time, he could give her what she needed. Tonight, he knew that was a good time.

'Come on. You know how to dance, don't you?' Enzo opened the top buttons of his shirt, a symbol of his determination to let loose for a little while.

'Of sorts. I'm used to a more formal setting.'

She didn't look comfortable as they approached the party area. He supposed someone of her standing had been strictly ballroom rather than disco up until now. In contrast, he'd done his best to avoid those kinds of stuffy events. Without his parents' influence he hadn't really known how to navigate them, and, he supposed, he hadn't wanted to be judged, sneered at. It had been easier to arrange his own casual gatherings where he was king and didn't have to worry about ever being seen as a failure in some fashion.

At least he knew how to relax, move to the rhythm and feel the music. Thaleia, on the other hand, couldn't have looked more uptight. He didn't want her to feel uncomfortable or look foolish. All she needed was a lesson in how to move.

He put a hand at her waist. 'You just need to relax your body. Be fluid.'

She tried to follow his instruction, but she still looked awkward. Like a stick trying to bend in the wind, rather than a blade of grass swaying.

'I feel stupid,' she said, turning to leave, but Enzo grabbed her hand and pulled her back.

'Let me show you.' He stood behind her, her back to his chest, his arm around her waist. 'Now, close your eyes and just pretend your bones have melted.'

'What?' She attempted to turn around, but he held her fast.

'I promise, if this doesn't work we can leave, but I want you to at least try to relax.'

He could almost feel her rolling her eyes at him as she muttered, 'OK.'

The music playing now had more of a salsa beat, which meant getting even closer than they already were. He'd fancied himself as a dance instructor before he'd realised the effect Thaleia's body pressed tightly against him would have. Doing his best to focus on the music, on the rhythm, rather than the quickstep his heart was doing.

He tucked his head in next to hers, and they swayed to the music, their bodies as one. A sultry, intimate dance that might not have won many awards in a professional setting, but that ticked all of his boxes.

All too soon, the song was over, and a different, more up-tempo beat sounded, ending their moment. The crowd began jumping, fists pumping in the air, bouncing around to the music.

'I think that's our cue to leave,' Enzo suggested, not wanting to push her too far out of her comfort zone.

They were making their way back to their seats when a too enthusiastic dancer jostled into them, knocking Thaleia off balance. Before Enzo could grab her, she gave a gasp, then she was falling, splashing into the swimming pool. Everything stopped. The music came to an abrupt end, and everyone rushed over to stare as Thaleia spluttered, coming up for air. Her make-up was running, her hair stuck to her skin, and her dress completely submerged in the water.

Enzo could see she was struggling to hold back the tears as everyone witnessed her humiliation, and he wanted to protect her whatever way he could. He did the one thing that came to mind and jumped right in beside her. The best way to get over an embarrassment like this was to embrace it, then people forgot it was even an issue. So he grabbed her into his hold and carried on dancing. Twirling her around and making a joke of it until the music came back on and people started whooping and cheering them on.

'Just go with it,' he whispered, lifting her legs around his waist so he could lead.

'You're mad,' she said, smiling, so he knew his plan had worked to an extent. The focus would be on his antics now rather than her misfortune.

To both their amusement, the partygoers thought dancing fully clothed in the water was the greatest idea ever and soon joined them.

Couples holding hands and jumping in beside them, until the pool was swarming with dancers splashing around them. It wasn't long before everyone forgot Thaleia's mishap.

'Come on, let's get out of these wet things.' Once he'd decided that they'd proved themselves fun enough for one evening, he waded back to the pool steps, still carrying Thaleia around his waist, her arms wrapped around his neck.

He set her down, water cascading down both of their bodies, but his interest solely on hers. As she wrung the water from her hair and her dress, he could see the material was almost transparent. Clinging to every curve of her body, the fabric moulded around her full breasts and left almost nothing to the imagination.

Enzo grabbed the jacket he'd discarded earlier and wrapped it around her to preserve her modesty.

'Thanks, Enzo. For everything.' Thaleia flashed him a watery smile.

'No problem. Accidents happen. It's how we deal with them that defines us.' Ironic coming from someone whose life had been completely upended by his parents' accident, and who had yet to deal with it properly.

'Enzo, darling. I see you're bringing your usual chaotic energy to my party.' Irida appeared, surveying the scene of revellers thrashing around in her pool.

He held his hand up. 'I can't help it if I'm a trendsetter. It was just a bit of fun, but now I'm afraid we've ruined Thaleia's outfit. Is there somewhere she can dry off, and perhaps find a change of clothes?'

'You poor dear. Enzo is such a bad influence. I had hoped, by the way he was talking about you the other day, that he might have settled down, but I see now he's the same incorrigible devil he always was.' Irida pinched Enzo's cheek playfully, making it impossible to protest what she'd said lest he seemed rude. He also didn't want Thaleia to think that settling down was on the cards for him.

Although he was a bit discombobulated at present, he was still sure he wasn't the man Thaleia needed. She remained silent during the exchange, which was worrying in itself. It was likely she was regretting ever agreeing to come to this shindig. He knew he was. All it had done was push them physically closer together and remind him of the attraction towards her that stubbornly refused to dissipate. As for her, the evening had no doubt shown her that side of him he'd been trying to keep at bay around her. Although that might not prove a bad thing when he needed to keep some distance between them.

Thaleia began to shiver.

'Don't let me keep you out here. The guest room is at the top of the stairs, last room on the left. You'll find some clean towels in the en suite bathroom, and there are some laundered clothes in the wardrobe from past guests. Help yourself. Feel free to stay the night if you'd prefer.'

'That won't be necessary—'

'I really don't think—'

Enzo and Thaleia shot down the idea at the same time, but Irida was already striding away from them.

'If you can't beat them…' she said, just before jumping into the pool, leaving her wig bobbing on the surface.

'The tiara!' Thaleia cried out.

'Don't worry. I'm sure her security will be right in after,' Enzo predicted, just as two burly men in black dived in to retrieve the jewels. He could see from here that the necklace was still around Irida's neck however, as she raved with the young crowd welcoming her to the new watery dance floor.

'You really do lead a strange life,' Thaleia said with a sigh as they turned and walked back towards the house.

'So you keep telling me.' Although he was beginning to see that himself now.

The settled existence Alex had chosen was beginning to hold more appeal day by day. Enzo was even beginning to wonder if it was jealousy that kept him from reaching out, or a denial that deep down that domestic life was what he might be craving too.

CHAPTER EIGHT

THALEIA FOLLOWED ENZO upstairs to the room Irida had directed them to, wishing she could change into her nightclothes, curl up in bed and forget everything that had happened. Her *own* bed, of course. While she appreciated the eccentric woman's hospitality, she'd no desire to remain here a moment longer than necessary.

First, though, she needed to change into something that wasn't completely transparent and furthering her humiliation every second she remained wearing it.

'You go on into the bathroom to dry off, and I'll see what I can find us to wear in the wardrobe.' Enzo let them into the guest room, which was likely the same size as her entire villa. At least it gave them plenty of space to avoid any further physical contact between them.

Every time he'd pressed against her tonight, her body had been in flames. Even while submerged in the pool. She should have insisted on leaving as soon as she'd accomplished what she'd come here for, having seen Irida wearing her work. Then she might not have ended up in this current predicament.

Thaleia perched on the edge of the sunken bath recalling the moment she'd been nudged into the pool. The humiliation she'd felt as she'd resurfaced to find all eyes watching her. Reliving that awful day in the church when Makis had failed to turn up and she'd had to face the gossiping wedding guests as the reality had set in. She'd wanted to run out tonight in floods of tears, just as she had that day. It was only thanks to Enzo that she had one less trauma to keep her awake at night. He'd turned her mortification into a party.

She hugged his jacket tighter around her. It smelled of him. Expensive and spicy. Enzo made her feel safe. As though he could take all of her problems away. Then again, the sort of man who could turn any occasion into an excuse to party wasn't exactly the reliable type she needed right now.

Reluctantly, she peeled off his jacket. Horrified by what she saw when she spotted her reflection in the mirror. Never mind the flattened hair and streaked make-up, it was the transparent nature of her outfit that had her blushing. Thank goodness for Enzo stepping in again to cover her up, and not even a flirty comment to boot. Though she'd be lying if she said that didn't bother her. She still wanted to think she was as attractive to him as he was to her, so this chemistry between them wasn't all in her head. Even if they couldn't do anything about it.

Perhaps she'd read too much into it all. He was an incredible flirt. Regardless that she was the only one who'd had his attention tonight. She'd half imagined that, once they'd got here and he'd made the introductions, he'd revert to type and find himself a bevy of beauties to spend the night with, but he'd been a gentleman all night.

So why did she have a sense of disappointment that nothing more had happened between them? Likely because the couple of kisses they'd shared had spoken of wonders waiting if they let things go any further.

She moved to the sink and splashed cold water over her face, removing the last traces of her make-up. Stripping off her wet clothes left her shivering and she quickly wrapped a towel around her before going back into the bedroom.

Just in time to see Enzo's bare backside as he stepped into a pair of board shorts.

'Sorry, I didn't realise—' She hovered in the bathroom doorway, not sure whether to go back in and pretend it had never happened or carry on. Flustered by the sight of his lean, muscular body, naked for a fleeting moment, but which would live for a long time in her memory.

'My fault. I thought I could change before you came back out.' He turned around, flashing his bare chest now as he pulled a white silk shirt over his head.

'Is there something for me?' She averted her gaze and focused on the clothes strewn on the bed.

'Nothing tasteful,' he laughed. 'I think the guests here spend most of their time by the pool. There are a few bikinis and cover-alls, but I did find a pair of shorts.' He held up the teeniest pair of shorts Thaleia had ever seen. She'd be lucky if they covered her backside.

'Maybe if I put it all on at once, I might manage to preserve some modesty.' Thaleia gathered the gaudy, skimpy clothes into her arms and prepared to disappear into the bathroom again.

'You only have to wear them to the limo. No one will see you.'

'I hope not.' It was bad enough Enzo was here to witness it, on top of everything else that had happened tonight. Goodness knew what was in store for her at her parents' party if this was anything to go by. Once that was over, she'd hide herself back in her shop where she was comfortable and safe from embarrassing herself any further.

The lime-green bikini just about fitted over her assets, but she was happier once she donned the paisley-patterned cover-all over it. The hot-pant shorts gave little extra coverage, but she no longer felt as exposed as she had been in her waterlogged dress. There wasn't much she could do about her hair, which was hanging limply around her shoulders.

Enzo was folding their clothes into a neat, wet pile as she re-entered the bedroom.

'Very domesticated,' she said with a grin.

'I have my moments.'

'You cook, you tidy… I think you'd make someone a great husband.' She was teasing, but her words had the opposite effect of her intention to make him smile.

Instead, his face was dark. Unreadable. 'I don't think so. You've seen for yourself how terrible I'd be taking care of anyone other than myself. I'm too selfish to be a family man.'

'Nonsense.' Thaleia surprised them both with her outburst, but she wouldn't hear him say another derogatory thing about himself. She might have believed it once, but that was before she got to know the man behind the reputation.

She took a step closer and stroked his cheek with her hand. 'You've done nothing but take care of me since we met.'

He took her hand and kissed her palm before

letting go. 'That's very sweet of you to say, but everything has still been on my terms, hasn't it? The picnic, coming here, were things I wanted to happen. I'm just very good at getting people to do what I want.'

Thaleia should have been annoyed, but she wasn't. He was working too hard to convince her, and himself, that he wasn't reliable. Yet he hadn't had anything to gain by introducing her to Irida or getting her to wear the necklace to give the business more credibility. All things he'd done solely to help Thaleia. Not to mention jumping straight into the pool to save her blushes.

'That may be so, but I know there's another side to you, Enzo. A caring, generous nature, which, for some reason, you're too afraid to acknowledge.' The part of him she was drawn to, but that also terrified her, because she knew he was all wrong for her.

'So caring I couldn't take carc of my little sister when she needed me most and went partying at university instead.' He gave a bitter laugh, which gave Thaleia chills. 'I was a failure as a son and a brother.'

His face was contorted in pain and anger directed at himself. Mostly, she suspected, through grief he hadn't processed properly.

'What age were you, Enzo? Seventeen? Eighteen? It was a lot for anyone to take on at any age, but you were young and grieving too.'

'You know, Irida reminded me of how self-absorbed I am. It was the same when we moved to England. I should have been there to help Bea through the grief of losing our parents, but I couldn't face it. I just drank and partied so I didn't have to think about it.' The pain on his face hurt just to look at. This was the real Enzo. A grieving teenager who'd used alcohol and women to block out the reality of losing his parents. The question was whether or not he would ever face the loss and how it had affected him and his sister, or carry on pretending it had never happened.

'Maybe you're right and your behaviour was questionable at times. None of us are perfect. I think you've probably been dealing with some post-traumatic stress or are not dealing with it at all. That's the problem. But the man you're describing isn't the Enzo Capelli I know. All I can say is that you've been very kind to me and I am happy you're here.' It wasn't until Enzo had crashed into her life a few days ago that she'd realised how lonely she was on the island. He'd been supportive and provided a companionship she hadn't known she'd been missing.

She had hidden away from the world to lick her wounds after her failed wedding day, but that had meant cutting all ties with everyone she knew and loved. It might have saved her from getting hurt, from anyone letting her down again, but just working and existing hadn't made her as happy as she'd thought.

There was a difference between not relying on a man to give her life meaning and having a man who enhanced it. Thaleia had limited the path her life would take by cutting everyone out of it.

In an ideal world she'd be married with children, probably still working, but with her family taking priority. Because that was what would have made her happy. Her ex ruined all that. Not only by sabotaging their plans for the future, but by ensuring she was too scared to want that again with someone else. So she'd accepted life as a spinster, living out in the middle of nowhere, because it was safe. With no surprises. At least until Enzo had come along.

He'd made life exciting again. Unpredictable. And while that was scary at times, she had enjoyed it too. When she was with Enzo, she felt like the old Thaleia, before her world had come crashing down around her. The Thaleia who knew how to have fun without worrying about getting hurt. Who thought there might just be something for her beyond the walls of the family home where love was nothing but a fairy tale. She'd been loath to admit it, but she still believed. It was who she put that belief in that caused her problems.

No matter what Enzo said, tonight he'd gone above and beyond to help her out. Those weren't the actions of someone who was selfish, who didn't care about anyone other than himself. Nor a self-absorbed teenager who couldn't be bothered to do something that didn't benefit him personally. This was a man who could be relied upon to do the right thing. Who looked out for someone he hardly knew without expecting anything in return.

Exactly the reason her defences were at their lowest. Catnip for a woman who'd been let down so publicly and cruelly and who'd been on her own too long.

Right now, this man who'd taken care of her tonight was hurting and she desperately wanted him to feel better.

She took his face in her hands. 'I think you're being too hard on yourself, Enzo. I know you're a good man at heart. I wish you knew it too.'

He gave her a sad half-smile that melted her heart. Acting on impulse, she leaned forward and placed her lips on his. She got the feeling she wasn't the only lonely one here, that he needed some display of affection, and in that moment she wanted to be the one to give it. However, she hadn't accounted for what that gesture would awaken inside her. Inside both of them. Instead of pulling away the instant she kissed him, she lingered there, enjoying the feel of him on her lips. Then Enzo did the unexpected and kissed her back with a ferocious passion that stole the breath from her lungs.

Her head was dizzy, her knees weak, but the rest of her body alert and compliant.

His hot mouth on hers was as firm and confident as his hand now circling her waist, pulling her flush to his hard body. The blood rushing in her head obliterated all reasons she'd told herself numerous times why this couldn't happen, and let her revel in the kiss. In the sexy, lust-filled moment making her feel wanted, desired. No longer alone or rejected.

Intoxicating.

Enzo moved his hand down to cup her backside. A possessive move that only fired the blood in her veins further. Thaleia realised she wanted this, needed it. Not only was it an ego boost to know she had this effect on him, that she was desirable, but it told her something more about herself. That moving away, focusing on work and avoiding relationships because she was scared of getting hurt, didn't mean she wasn't missing certain elements. Only now was she aware that physical intimacy was something that had been missing. And Enzo seemed very keen to provide.

Panting breath, pulse racing, Enzo's mouth and tongue working overtime to seduce her, it was overwhelming, but she surrendered to it all. Letting the moment take her, carry her away, and forgetting everything except how her body was reacting to him. Arousal her new master.

Then Enzo pulled away, and she came crashing back down to earth. Abandoned and humiliated all over again.

'I can't…' He looked almost disgusted by what had happened, even though they kept finding themselves in this position. Albeit every kiss taking them a little further, that attraction refusing to abate.

So she couldn't understand why he was saying otherwise.

'What is it?' Thaleia staggered back a few steps, off balance because of the ferocity of the kiss and the sudden way it had ended. Leaving her a little disoriented as well as confused.

'Your brother… I just can't.' His explanation was far from explanatory or satisfactory.

'My brother?' she spat incredulously. It was the last thing she'd expected him to say.

If he'd decided he didn't want to get involved with someone on the rebound from a failed relationship, or even if he'd said that she ultimately wasn't his type, it might have been easier to accept than using her brother as an excuse.

Enzo held his head in his hands. 'Alex is my friend. You're his sister.'

'And?' It hadn't seemed to bother him before.

'It just doesn't feel right.'

Thaleia huffed out a breath. 'It felt pretty right to me. Unless I'm completely wrong and that didn't feel good for you.'

She cringed with every word when it seemed as though she was begging him to tell her that she was worthy of him after all.

'No. It did. It's just—'

'I'm Alex's sister. Alex, who, by your own admission, you've grown apart from. Who you called boring. The brother I had when you came looking for me on the island and when you kissed me before.' Her sudden anger was a direct response to the embarrassment swamping her, to knowing that he didn't want her now he knew he could have her.

'I know, but—'

'It doesn't matter. Can we go home, please? I'm cold, wet and tired.' Not to mention suddenly teary. All she wanted to do was crawl into bed and hide away from the world again. Pull the blanket over her head and pretend this had never happened and that Enzo Capelli didn't exist.

'Thaleia—'

She didn't wait to hear any more excuses, or see pity in his eyes, because it was beginning to feel like her wedding day all over again. Thankfully, this time, her rejection had been conducted in private at least.

Thaleia grabbed her wet clothes from the bed, and wrenched the bedroom door open. Only to be met with Irida on the other side. Her wig was now wet and slightly askew, and she'd changed into another diaphanous gown. Minus the wings, but with her accessories still intact.

'I was just coming to check on you two. I hope I wasn't disturbing anything?' She glanced at Thaleia, then at Enzo, who was standing some distance behind her.

'Not at all,' he said. 'Thank you for the use of the room, and the dry clothes.'

'Don't let me spoil your fun. As I said, you're free to stay the night.' Her gaze lingered on Thaleia, and she wondered if the effects of their tryst were written all over her face. Along with the devastation that Enzo didn't want her after all.

She should have been glad he'd had the sense to end things before they went too far, but her only thought was that he didn't want her either. Just like her ex. And it was her own fault she was upset. She'd known from the beginning that Enzo was dangerous for her welfare.

'Thank you for your hospitality, but I have to get back to make sure my shop is open tomorrow. I have commitments.' She bundled past

Irida, worried she'd make even more of a scene if she stayed.

The knowing look Irida exchanged with Enzo didn't go unnoticed though. As if there was some sort of secret between them that Thaleia wasn't privy to. She wouldn't put it past him to have had a fling with the older woman at some point, when they were like two peas in a pod. Perhaps they were friends with benefits and she'd got in the way of their usual arrangement. A ridiculous notion, maybe, but she was too upset to think clearly. Especially when she'd just been rejected by a man whose reputation was built on the number of women he'd casually slept with and discarded.

What was it about her that was so repellent that he didn't want to add her to his list of conquests?

Enzo was sorry the night had ended on a low point when he'd really tried his best to make Thaleia feel part of it. It was his fault, of course, for giving in to temptation, again, then pulling right back. Naturally, she was upset and confused, and he'd done his best to explain why he couldn't let things go any further. Only stopping short from telling her about the pact he had with Alex because there was no way she would understand it. In fact, she'd probably be humiliated all over again if she found out that her brother thought she was incapable of being in control of her own life. Then she'd be mad at them both for making decisions on her behalf, and treating her as though she weren't a person in her own right.

Looking back now, he knew that pact had been immature, but still, he knew if he hooked up with Thaleia, Alex would never forgive him. Although they'd become distant, Enzo was hoping that some day they'd find their way back into one another's lives. If he crossed that line with Thaleia, he knew there would be no way back with Alex. He was protective of his little sister, just as Enzo was with Bea. Breaking that pact would mean Alex never trusting him again.

Apart from anything else, he was concerned that the closeness he had shared with her up until last night could make things tricky for him personally. The women he usually slept with were virtual strangers, people he would never see again. Neither party expected more than one night of having fun. There were no emotional entanglements, complications or guilt involved. With Thaleia, all three were involved.

He knew he couldn't be with her long term and it didn't seem fair to lead her on. Someone like Thaleia didn't sleep with a man and just forget about it. As far as he knew, the last man she'd been with was the man she'd thought she was going to marry. She didn't deserve someone else who had no intention of sticking around.

The car journey was not a pleasant one.

Thaleia was sitting as far away from him as possible in the back of the car, and he knew, if he didn't fix things now, this could be the last time he saw her. Although he'd be moving on soon, he didn't want things to end this way. With her thinking that she'd done something wrong.

'Remind me when your parents' party is again?' He attempted some small talk to bridge the gap and gauge her current feelings towards him.

'A week from today, but don't feel obliged to go. I'm not going to force you.' Arms folded, she turned back away from him to stare out of the window.

OK, so she pretty much despised him and wanted nothing more to do with him.

He didn't want this to be her everlasting memory of him and their time together. Nor did he want her brother to find out he'd led her on in some way, then dropped her like a hot potato.

'I said I would return the favour. I know you wanted some moral support.'

Thaleia snorted. 'I think I can do without it, thanks.'

'Listen, Thaleia, I want to be with you, I do. But we both know it wouldn't work out. It would just be asking for trouble. I'll be moving on soon and there's nothing to be gained from getting romantically involved right now.'

Except for the obvious. Kissing Thaleia was enough to set him on fire and he could only imagine what it would be like to take the next step. However, it was the likely aftermath that prevented him from acting on that impulse. The fallout with Alex, dealing with his own guilt and the possibility of hurting Thaleia by using her as just another notch on his bedpost made a one-night stand seem like going back to his selfish ways. Because that was all it could ever be. Anything more than a physical connection was a relationship, and those didn't work out well for him.

Apart from a long line of women who'd expected more, regardless of his reputation, he had an estranged sister and best friend. All evidence that he wasn't the man Thaleia needed in her life right now.

'I know,' she sighed. 'It was just that feeling of being rejected that got to me. Goodness knows I've had enough of that for one lifetime.'

He understood why she was upset. Even kissing him must have been a huge step for her, leaving herself vulnerable like that, and he'd made things worse.

Enzo slid along the seat and turned her face to look at him. 'It wasn't you. It wasn't even me.

I just don't think it would be a good idea to let this develop any further.'

If he had any hope of ever seeing her again, of salvaging things with Alex at some point, he had to show some restraint. Not least for his own sake. Tonight had shown him that there were feelings already there towards Thaleia. He'd never gone out of his way for anyone as he had for her by visiting Irida before the party and asking her for the favour. By sleeping together, moving the relationship he and Thaleia had already cultivated on to that next level, he would only be inviting drama. For her, and himself.

They already had a connection through Alex, and these past few days had seen an emotional one develop between him and Thaleia. He didn't usually bring emotions into the bedroom beyond having a good time because he didn't want to be responsible for someone else's happiness other than physically. In bed he didn't have a problem, it was out of it the trouble began.

'I didn't have you down as the sensible type, Enzo.' The corners of Thaleia's mouth were curved upward, hopefully a sign that she was beginning to forgive him.

Given what had nearly happened tonight, he should really haul anchor and move on, but he owed it to Thaleia to be there for her parents' party. He'd seen how nervous she'd been tonight, how much it had taken for her to come and mingle with virtual strangers. He could only imagine how facing her family and friends again was going to feel. She needed him. Or at least the selfless version of him who simply wanted to help her. Give her the support he wasn't sure she was getting from anyone else. As far as he knew no one had come to check on her out here after that traumatic day in church. He'd come to know her enough these past days to see how vulnerable and fragile she was beneath that tough exterior.

'I have my moments. So, am I forgiven, then?' He batted his eyelashes at her, trying to get them back to where they'd been before chemistry had taken over from common sense.

'I suppose so. I do need my trophy date for next Saturday.' It was her turn to inject a little humour back into the conversation. Something they were both more comfortable with than the deep and meaningful stuff they'd been dealing with. Though she didn't fool him. It was obvious how much he'd hurt her, and he reckoned he owed her a little confidence boost. He was going to go all out to make sure she felt supported and appreciated on Saturday.

'I'll make sure to bring my A game to the party and make everyone green with envy.'

Thaleia pursed her lips. 'I'm not sure I want *that*, Enzo. Just be yourself and be there for me.'

'I can do that. I think.' *I hope.*

CHAPTER NINE

'YOU KNOW, THIS ISN'T the sort of party I usually go to,' Enzo whispered as they walked up to Thaleia's parents' home. They'd anchored the yacht near Piraeus, the port closest to Athens, taken a tender to the harbour and a limo to get from there.

Likely because of the warm weather, the guests had spilled out onto the lawn, sipping drinks to the sound of the band that must have been set up somewhere out back.

'Oh, I've seen the kind of parties you're used to and they are something else.' Thaleia was still recovering from it. This time around she'd got over her public embarrassment pretty quickly but it was the private moment when Enzo had pushed her away she was having trouble dealing with. As well as her reaction to the incident.

She'd just been so lost in the kiss, it hurt to think it hadn't had the same effect on him. Ultimately, she knew it had been for the best. It would have made things awkward between them for tonight, and probably would have left her feeling worse if she'd slept with him and he'd moved on. At least when that time came she would know he wasn't leaving because of her. She would have no reason to feel sorry for herself. Enzo had been the mature, responsible one that night. It was possible that her brother had been a valid reason for him putting a stop to things before they got out of control. If he wanted to reconcile with his friend, she doubted hooking up with his friend's little sister at a party was the right way to go about it.

Enzo had been the one to patch things up before they'd gone their separate ways too. If he hadn't, she would have found herself here alone, and that was a terrifying prospect. Especially when she could see her mother gliding across the lawn towards them. Dressed in an elegant cream trouser suit, she was the visual opposite to Irida, but nonetheless impressive.

'Thaleia, darling, it's so good to see you.' She kissed her daughter on both cheeks, all the while looking Enzo up and down. Assessing his worth both financially and socially, no doubt.

'You too, Mama. This is Enzo Capelli.' Thaleia made the introductions and watched her mother be seduced as he kissed her hand.

'It's a pleasure to meet you, Mrs Galatis.'

'Helena, please.'

Thaleia didn't think she'd ever seen her mother blush before, and found herself irrationally teed off as Enzo and her mother made eyes at one another. She'd asked him to charm her parents, to divert their attention from her. Still, it stung to see him flirt with someone else.

'Where's Papa?' she asked, keen to get the introductions over all at once.

'He's holding court at the back of the house. Why don't I take you to meet Nicholas, Enzo?' Her mother threaded her arm through Enzo's and began walking around the house, leaving Thaleia trailing behind.

'Sounds good.' Enzo at least had the grace to flash her an apologetic look as her mother paraded him around the garden.

'Thaleia tells me you're an old friend of Alex's?' It showed how much interest they showed in their children's lives when her mother didn't remember the summers Alex had stayed with Enzo.

'Yes, we went to university together. I haven't seen much of him recently though.' The sadness of that matter was there in his tone, even though Enzo made out that Alex's new life was too mundane for him. Thaleia had a feeling, given half the chance, he'd have Alex back in his life in a heartbeat.

He talked about him too much to not care, and he was afraid that getting involved with her would upset Alex in some way. That meant he was hoping for a reunion at some point. As much as he tried to convince everyone he was happy being a bachelor on his yacht, it was clear Enzo missed his friend. It had also been noticeable that he wanted his sister back in his life but was afraid she wouldn't want to get to know him. He needed people in his life, loved ones, but he'd been pretending for so long that he didn't, he'd even convinced himself.

'He's devoted himself to little Georgios. Wouldn't even come out to celebrate his parents' wedding anniversary. Can you imagine such a thing?' Her mother tutted, but Thaleia thought Alex was the lucky one, the brave one, who wouldn't take part in this charade.

This wasn't a celebration of marriage, of a long-lasting love between their parents. It was an excuse for a social event. For her parents to show off and make people believe they had the strongest relationship amongst their peers. Only she and Alex knew differently. She'd hand it to her parents: they were very good actors. Excellent at putting on a good show.

'He's being a good parent and putting his child first,' Thaleia muttered as she trailed behind the new happy couple, though she knew her mother wouldn't pick up on that slight against her. Mrs Galatis prided herself on being an excellent mother without ever consulting her children to find out if it was true.

Thaleia supposed they'd never been denied anything growing up, had had a good education and start in life. The main thing that had been lacking in their lives had been a real sense of love. Their parents, though united when it came to business, or social events, were not a typical loving couple. Separate bedrooms and lives behind closed doors, which Thaleia had taken as the norm, were not how her friends' parents behaved.

Eventually she came to a realisation that they'd never loved one another, and had merely married as some sort of business merger. Their two families coming together to create the ultimate power couple. Certainly, they worked well as a team and had proved a successful match when it came to business. However, there had been little warmth between them, and Thaleia had vowed to marry for love, rather than money, when considering her future.

So far, that hadn't turned out well.

'Ah, the prodigal daughter returns.' Her father spotted her, completely bypassing her mother and Enzo to come and hug her. The crowd of people he'd been talking to watching with interest.

It was always difficult to tell at these things if

people were curious about her because she was the daughter of the well-known couple, or if it was because they knew about her being jilted at the altar. As though they were watching for signs of why things had gone so wrong. Waiting for her to have some kind of emotional breakdown to explain why her fiancé had decided he didn't want to be with her for ever after all.

'It's nice to see you, Papa.' Thaleia hugged him, realising that, despite all their faults, they were her parents and she had missed them. She only wished Alex were here too.

'And who is this your mother has got her claws into?' her father asked, assessing Enzo in his own way. Eyes sweeping over him, perhaps wondering if he was good enough for his daughter, or if he'd be another let-down.

In a way, Thaleia felt bad for deceiving them, but she didn't have the energy for her mother's matchmaking tonight. It was easier to simply pretend she and Enzo were a couple, and fake a break-up at a later date. Hopefully she could relax a little knowing she wasn't being judged by bachelors who might have been lined up to see if she was a suitable partner for them too.

'Enzo Capelli.' Enzo extracted himself from her mother's clutches to shake her father's hand. The sort of confident handshake she knew her father would approve of.

'Ah, yes. I have heard the name before.' Mr Galatis nodded approvingly, no doubt remembering that Enzo had his own personal fortune and wouldn't be some sort of gold-digger. Another problem Thaleia had had in the past when dating—men only interested in inveigling themselves into the family for possible financial gain. Thankfully, she'd figured that out for herself on those occasions when the men hadn't been with her because they'd loved her. She only wished she'd been as savvy when it came to her ex too, and realised he couldn't promise to love her for ever. Not even on their wedding day.

'Happy anniversary to you both,' Enzo said politely, clearly on his best behaviour.

She had to commend him for agreeing to come to this. Especially after their last social outing together. He could easily have decided this was more trouble than it was worth when he had nothing to gain from it. It wasn't as though he were trying to get her into bed by playing the nice guy. She reckoned this was just who he was behind the extrovert façade.

'Thank you. Now come get a drink and meet everyone.' Her father clapped an arm around Enzo's shoulders and steered him towards the group he'd been chatting to. Clearly, he'd been deemed worthy of attention. Although Thaleia was a little peeved, it should take the heat off her if they thought she was indeed dating a suitable match.

The irony wasn't lost on her that the very reason Enzo didn't want to be with her was who her family was.

He surprised her by reaching back and taking her hand. 'Come and meet everyone, Thaleia.' Making sure to include her, where her parents had failed.

It was only her sense of duty as their daughter that had compelled her to come at all. Unlike Alex, she had no real excuse to keep her away from home. She supposed coming back for a party, with lots of other people, was slightly better than coming back on her own, where the sole focus would be on her and her failure to secure a husband. Sometimes she felt like the narrator in a Jane Austen novel.

Along with her mother, she joined the others, wishing she'd had time to grab a drink first.

'We were just discussing your ex, Makis,' one of the other middle-aged men of the group said without a hint of self-awareness. As though even the mention of his name wouldn't upset her, never mind that there was more gossip surrounding her.

'Oh?' she said simply, grateful for Enzo, who moved to stand next to her, a reassuring arm around her waist. Bracing her for whatever was about to come.

'Yes, he's marrying that daughter of Athos. What's her name?' He clicked his fingers, trying to remember, as though that was the most important detail of his revelation.

Her legs threatened to give way with the news, and Enzo tightened his grip on her.

'Evangeline,' her mother offered.

'You knew, and didn't tell me?' Thaleia gasped, the betrayal twofold.

'I didn't think it was worth mentioning. He's history, darling, and not a pleasant one. Why should you care when you've got this handsome man now?' Her mother fluttered her eyelashes at Enzo, but that still wasn't the most sickening thing for Thaleia.

Makis hadn't been averse to marrying, he'd been averse to marrying *her*. It was difficult not to take that personally. That there had been something lacking in her in some way that he'd decided last minute he didn't want to spend the rest of his life with her. Though, apparently, he had no qualms about being with someone else.

It hurt like hell, but she couldn't exactly say that when she was supposed to be loved up with Enzo.

'I'm a lucky lady,' she said through the wave

of nausea crashing over her, kissing Enzo on the cheek for extra measure.

If they had been together, she probably wouldn't have cared. However, finding this out after Enzo's rejection the other night wasn't going to do her self-confidence any good. She was beginning to wonder if anyone would ever want her, or if she was going to live out the rest of her days alone.

The thought wasn't a happy one. As content as she had been working and living away from home, she wasn't sure she wanted that life for ever. There was still that hope that she'd find someone who loved her enough to marry her, and start a family, but that was looking unlikelier by the moment. The last two men she'd kissed had both rejected her, and, like Makis, Enzo was probably going to move on to someone else sooner rather than later. At this rate he'd be married before she was.

'Your ex was just a practice run for the real thing. Isn't that right, Thaleia?' Enzo dropped a kiss on her lips, which managed to both excite her body and draw attention from everyone else. She supposed that meant they'd succeeded in their mission to convince everyone they were in a happy, stable relationship. When nothing could be further from the truth.

'Tell me how you two met. Thaleia has been

very quiet on the subject. I didn't even know she was seeing anyone.' Her mother was sipping her champagne and watching their interaction.

Thaleia couldn't help but think she'd sussed out that this was an elaborate ruse. Having everyone find out that she'd faked a romance with Enzo would be humiliating, and cement her place as the biggest loser in love in Greek history.

Thankfully Enzo volunteered the story because Thaleia didn't think she could lie so convincingly. It was unnerving that he could.

'It was love at first sight. I commissioned Thaleia to make some jewellery for me. She showed me around the island, and we got to know each other. She's a very special woman.' Enzo looked at her as though he were a man in love. A convincing act that made even her flush.

'Ah, your "business". Tell me how that's going for you, Thaleia.' The sneer in her father's voice wasn't unexpected. She'd heard his scathing opinion before she'd left home. None of it positive or complimentary. He hadn't thought it a valuable use of her time. Which, in his opinion, would be better spent looking for a husband who could provide her with the kind of lifestyle she'd been used to. In that way, they would have seen Enzo as a perfect candidate for the position. She knew better. He'd made it very clear that he wasn't about to become anyone's husband, never mind a woman he regretted kissing time and time again.

'It's going well. We were at Irida Angelopoulos's party recently and she wore one of my designs. I'm hoping that will spark some new orders. I've already had some enquiries. Plenty to keep me busy.' She doubted she was ever going to make millions doing what she did, but if she made enough profit to live independently, she'd be happy enough with her lot. Not everything was about money. She valued happiness over that. Something she'd had a glimpse of at times when she'd been with Enzo, but wondered if she'd ever find on a long-term basis.

'What do you make of this, Enzo? Don't you think my daughter could be doing something more productive with her time? She doesn't need to work, to get her hands dirty. I've offered her countless positions in the company but she seems determined to waste her time making jewellery.'

Her father was talking to Enzo as though she weren't even there, showing no respect for her or her work. It wasn't anything new. Nicholas Galatis didn't believe anything other than his business deserved his interest. That didn't mean it wasn't galling when Thaleia had put her heart and soul into her venture.

'I think Thaleia is excellent at what she does, and it makes her happy. That's all that's important.' Enzo spoke up on her behalf, drawing a derisive snort from her father.

'I can see why you're so well suited. You're both dreamers.' Her father turned his back on them then to carry on talking with his friends, apparently deeming them unworthy of any more of his time.

'Is that such a bad thing, Papa? I am good at what I do, and it makes me happy. Isn't that what's important?' Her heart was pounding, her temperature rising, as she stood up for herself.

She'd always done what was expected of her, what her parents wanted, and that had included marrying the so-called 'right one', and none of it had made her happy. It was only since she'd hit absolute rock-bottom and begun to make a life of her own, independent from her family's influence, that she'd begun to feel something other than pain. Pride, contentment, things her work had brought back into her life, and she didn't care what anyone thought.

Her father slowly turned his head towards her. 'You're never going to make any money with that attitude.'

'Not everything in life is about money,' Enzo countered, showing, not only remarkable courage in speaking against her father, but a sense that he'd been doing some soul-searching himself.

'Says a man who lives on a superyacht.' Thaleia's father drew stifled laughter from the other party guests with his quip.

'Trust me, Mr Galatis, I'd give it all up if I thought I could be happy. Now, if you'll excuse us, I think we'll go and get some drinks.' Enzo looked at Thaleia for confirmation that was what she wanted to do and she nodded eagerly, taking his hand and moving away from the toxic group.

'Thanks,' Thaleia said once they were out of earshot. 'And sorry about that. I should have warned you what you were in for.'

'I can handle myself. I just didn't like your parents putting you down like that.' Enzo waved the bartender over at the makeshift bar that had been set up for the guests on the grounds, and ordered wine.

'I'm used to it. My father likes to be in control of everything. It doesn't sit well with him that I want to do my own thing.' She imagined that even if she'd wanted to go off into the corporate world, instead of being creative, he would have still had a problem because it wasn't what he wanted for her.

'I can see why he and Alex would have clashed so much. He told me they didn't get on very well. I understand now why he was so reluctant to go home in the holidays.' Enzo leaned on the bar as he recounted what he'd learned about her brother's relationship with her father.

'I always assumed he was having too much fun to come home.' She'd missed Alex. Always waiting for him to turn up on the doorstep for those big important holidays, but, more often than not, he'd spent them with Enzo. She'd been jealous at the thought he was partying in England while she was sitting in her room at home, waiting for him to visit.

'There was some of that going on too.' Enzo's grin said she hadn't been too far off the mark, but if Alex and her father had a better relationship she was sure he would've come home more often. She couldn't blame him for going away and forgetting all about them. That was the reason she'd moved to the island, after all. To forget.

'You know, I never saw how controlling my father was until I left home. When I started to make my own decisions and realised they were the complete opposite to what my parents wanted of me. In hindsight, Makis had been their choice. My mother kept pushing me towards him, and my father would invite him to the house so we saw one another all the time. There was a lot made about how he was perfect for me, and I believed it.'

'There's a lot of that going on in big families like ours. I can only imagine how hard my own mother would be pushing me for marriage if she were still here. She'd be horrified to find out about my lifestyle.'

'I suppose they really only want what's best for us, but I don't think that should include trampling over our own hopes and dreams.' Thaleia was beginning to realise that the reason she'd invested so much in her relationship with her ex was that she was constantly being told he was the right one. She'd become so used to doing everything her father wanted, she'd believed it.

Looking back, she wondered if she'd really been in love with Makis, or simply the idea of being married. Perhaps he'd realised that too at the last minute. She could honestly say that one kiss with Enzo was full of more passion than she'd ever shared with her ex in their years of being together.

It also dawned on her that Makis had never stood up for her the way Enzo had just now. There had been times when her father had belittled her in front of him the way he'd done tonight, and her ex had simply laughed along with him. Told her to lighten up if she got upset and confronted him about it. Making it her problem. Regardless that her father's behaviour had already caused one member of the family to distance himself from them.

'No. It shouldn't. I'm proud of you for challenging him.' Enzo held his glass of wine up and she clinked it with hers, feeling proud of herself for finally finding her feet, and her voice.

These past few days with Enzo had helped her discover who she was. With his support and encouragement she'd stopped hiding away, being afraid to let anyone into her life to hurt her again. She wasn't ready to lose him.

Enzo was being honest about the pride he'd felt when Thaleia had stood her ground and told her father she was happy with the simple life she'd made for herself. He was envious that she was content with so little, when he had so much yet didn't feel at all fulfilled. Still, it would be nice to have parents of any sort. If he had, he mightn't feel this emptiness inside that he could never quite manage to fill.

'I'm not sure it'll make any difference in the long run. He still thinks I'm a failure, and likely always will.' Thaleia's jubilant smile began to falter, and Enzo could see her confidence gradually ebb away, presumably knowing she could have that conversation time and time again and her father's opinion would never change.

She'd come on such a journey these last few days, perhaps even months, believing in herself more, that he hated to see her waver.

'Then it's just as well you and I know better, isn't it?' he said, doing his best to set her back on track.

'It's ridiculous that you, a virtual stranger, know me better than my own parents. I don't even know why I came here tonight. Alex had the right idea. At least he's not pretending any more.'

'What do you mean?'

'All this.' She gestured around her to the gathered guests. 'It's fake.'

'I don't understand, Thaleia.' He was confused about what wasn't real here, except the relationship they were trying to convince everyone they were in.

'This is an anniversary party for a couple who don't even love each other. It's all for show.' There was a growing hysteria in her voice, and Enzo laid a gentle hand on her arm to help her rein it in before she drew attention. He knew she'd regret causing any sort of a scene in the long run.

'Many married couples fall out of love, or just take one another for granted. It doesn't do them any harm to celebrate decades of marriage though. At least they're still together.' It was rare these days for couples to stay together for that length of time. In his opinion they deserved a medal. He couldn't imagine being with someone for years to come.

Thaleia shook her head. 'I wouldn't care if that's all it was, but I doubt they've ever loved one another. I think theirs was a business arrangement of some sort, a marriage of convenience, because it certainly wasn't a love match. It's a wonder Alex and I were ever born. I've never even seen them kiss. Perhaps having children was part of their deal, but, whatever it was, behind closed doors they're not such a united couple.'

Enzo supposed that hadn't made for a warm and fuzzy upbringing and explained some of the tension between family members. It also said a lot about why Alex had invested so much in being a good father. He likely wanted his son to grow up in a more loving environment. Only too late had Enzo realised that was what his parents had provided him. He hadn't appreciated it until they were gone and he'd had no one to look out for him. There had been times at university when he'd envied Alex his family, other times he'd been mad at him for not appreciating them. Now, having met them, he could understand why he kept his distance from his parents. Unfortunately, it was Thaleia who'd ended up caught in the crossfire. Left to deal with her parents' manipulation on her own.

He wasn't blind to the irony of his anger on her behalf when he was just as guilty as Alex in not seeing his sister's plight. After all, he'd practically abandoned Bea to deal with her grief alone too. At least now he could see that, in regretting his actions in his own grief, he might be able to make it up to his sister somehow. Confessing what he'd been going through too, admitting he'd been out of his depth and devastated by their parents' deaths, might help her to forgive him. Thanks to Thaleia, he was beginning to see that not everything had been as black and white as he'd seen it at the time.

It was a sign of Thaleia's strength too that she'd managed to extract herself from the toxicity of her family home and make a new life. She'd been through a lot and it would have been easier for her to simply acquiesce to her parents' wishes. Instead, she'd focused on what she wanted and fought for it. If he took a leaf out of her book, stopped running and faced up to what he was feeling, he might be able to salvage those relationships that still meant so much to him.

He hadn't thought he could admire her any more than he already did, but apparently there was still room inside him for a little more Thaleia worshipping.

'I never would have guessed your parents were anything other than a normal, loving couple.'

He glanced over at them now, Mr Galatis talking to his friends, and Mrs Galatis having words with the caterers. Clapping with the rest of the crowd as a giant cake was wheeled out complete with sparklers and confetti cannons going off. A real spectacle taking the focus off the fact the happy couple weren't standing anywhere near each other.

It was starting to look as though this was more of a social event than a celebration of their love after all.

'They deploy excellent distraction techniques,' Thaleia muttered as photographers appeared to capture the moment.

'In that case it's a wonder you ever wanted to get married yourself.' Enzo couldn't help but think that was what had put Alex off the idea of marriage. Though he'd never talked much about his parents, he'd been clear about one thing. That he would never marry. Thaleia might have been better off if she'd adopted the same tactic.

Thaleia looked at him with a faraway look in her eyes, as though she were back in that fairy tale. The one that said once she was married, she'd live happily ever after. Though they both knew that wasn't the case. Even in a loving marriage like the one his parents had had, no one was guaranteed that happy ending. Far from it in their case. If they hadn't died prematurely in such tragic circumstances, perhaps even Enzo might've believed in the fantasy himself. However, they were gone and nothing would bring them back.

'I suppose I was never told I had any option. I was going to get married and have a family. However, in my head I'd be marrying for love and nothing else. I wanted the perfect marriage, and a future with the man I loved. I suppose I didn't stop to question if that was Makis.' Thaleia stared into her glass as though the contents could somehow help her go back in time and change what had happened.

'And now?' Enzo knew first hand how trauma could alter a person's outlook, change the trajectory of their life. In a different world he might have had a nine-to-five office job, a wife and kids, instead of partying on a superyacht like an eternal bachelor.

Thaleia had already been changed by what had happened, otherwise she wouldn't have given up the luxury here to set up shop in the middle of nowhere.

It occurred to him that, though their pasts were as different as their lifestyles, they were both hiding from the world in their own way. While she had isolated herself in the hope of preventing further heartache, he hid in plain sight. Always partying, having fun on the outside, yet as lonely as Thaleia on the inside. They had more in common than they ever would have imagined.

She gave a heavy sigh as she contemplated his question. 'I wish I could say I was over it. That it's put me off the idea of marriage for life, but there's still a part of me that hopes to find "the one". I don't want to fake my way through life the way my parents have done. I want the real deal. I just think I'll be even more wary now about who I give my heart to.'

The pain in her eyes and the wobble in her smile hurt him to see. Yet he feared she was still leaving herself open to men like her ex who would take advantage of her dream to get what they wanted, then leave when faced with the idea of real commitment. Breaking her heart and her spirit all over again.

'You know, not every relationship has to lead to marriage. It's possible just to have fun with someone and not plan a future together for ever.'

'How's that working out for you?'

'Fine. I'm my own man. If I want to be with someone, I'll be with them. If I want to be on my own, so be it. I don't have to worry about feelings. Either theirs, or mine. I make sure everyone knows the score.' With the lifestyle he led it wasn't difficult to find women only interested in one night. The sort of people he met in clubs, invited back to his yacht, were all about having a good time with no expectation beyond that. Just how he liked it. Enzo left out that sense of loneliness that was creeping in more and more lately. She didn't need to hear that when he was trying to make her feel better.

Apparently Thaleia didn't agree, judging by the scowl on her face. 'That sounds like a very… empty life. No offence.'

'Any emptier than yours right now?' It wasn't meant as a low blow, but a reminder that she too was dodging commitment in her own way. At least he was still seeing people, getting out and enjoying life. Even if, deep down, he was as wounded as she was by the past.

Instead of getting angry at him for confronting her with the reality of her situation, Thaleia considered his words before finally saying, 'I guess not.'

Before they could get any deeper into analysing their attitudes to relationships, the band stopped playing, and Mr Galatis took the microphone.

'I want to thank everyone for coming here to celebrate forty years of marriage to my amazing wife.' He blew a kiss to Mrs Galatis, who was standing nearby playing the doting wife, blowing kisses back.

Thaleia was watching with a dark look on her face, tossing back her champagne.

'I don't know where I'd be if it weren't for you, baby. So, in honour of my undying love and devotion, and to mark the occasion, I'm going to sing our song.' Mr Galatis motioned to the band and began crooning an old love song, with a chorus of 'Aahs' from the impressed crowd. With two noticeable exceptions.

Thaleia made a vomit motion, clearly unimpressed with the display. 'I don't think I can stomach any more of this.'

'You don't have to. You're an adult, you know.' He knew she didn't like to go against her parents, but he'd seen for himself that they didn't respect her. It seemed unnecessary to put herself through this when it was clearly upsetting for her having to be part of the act.

'You're right. I've been the dutiful daughter. My part is done.' Thaleia set down her glass and stood a little straighter. 'So where else can we go at this time on a Saturday? It's too late for dinner, and too early for dancing.'

Enzo raised his eyebrows at her sudden want to go out somewhere with him. It was one thing faking being one another's date, but this was Thaleia actually expressing a desire to be with him. Until now he'd been the instigator of their adventures, having to convince her to go along with him. It showed how desperate she was to get out of here.

'Are you forgetting something? I have my own yacht, baby. We can party there all night if you want.' Thaleia needed somewhere safe to blow off steam. Tonight had been difficult for her, but the fact that she was even considering leaving marked a change in her. She was rebelling. Taking control of her life and Enzo was glad he was there to witness her blossoming. He'd be there for her tonight as a soundboard, a shoulder to lean on and whatever else she needed.

Enzo simply had to remember that kissing his best friend's sister was always a bad idea. Especially now that his time on the island was up.

CHAPTER TEN

THALEIA HAD NEVER seen the attraction in adrenaline-fuelled pursuits, but simply ditching her parents' party and taking off with Enzo was giving her a buzz she was sure was akin to bungee jumping or climbing a mountain. She felt invincible. Already searching for another high. Something she'd achieve simply by going back to Enzo's yacht rather than returning home.

After their last tryst at Irida's place, she knew he didn't want to start anything with her, so she felt safe. Not under pressure to think about doing anything more out of character by sleeping with someone she'd known for only a matter of days. She just wanted away from the mass delusion going on at her parents' place. Enzo's yacht seemed like the perfect spot to escape reality. After all, he'd been doing it for years.

'I hope you've got food on board. Women cannot live on champagne alone.' It had been such a short trip back to the yacht, and she'd been so caught up in her head about her parents' odd relationship, that it had barely registered.

Enzo had kept silent, clearly understanding her need to process everything. Not least, the fact that she'd finally stopped doing what was expected of her. OK, so she hadn't confronted her parents about anything, but this was a start. It felt as though there was a new, empowered Thaleia elbowing her way to the surface and she was here for it. So was Enzo.

He looked pleased with himself that she'd agreed to come back with him. Likely because it gave him some validation about the lifestyle she'd given him grief over. Tonight it seemed the perfect place to unwind and forget all her problems.

'I gave the crew the night off, but I'm sure the galley is well stocked. It might not be homemade pizza, but I'm sure we can find something. All that rebelling must have worked up your appetite.' Enzo thought she looked as though a weight had been lifted from her shoulders as they'd made their way back to the yacht.

'I don't know… I feel different. Lighter somehow,' she said once they were on board. 'That permanent knot in my stomach has gone. At least for now. Tomorrow might be different, but here, with you, I don't have any worries.'

He knew that feeling. Knew how being on

the yacht created a false reality, but he could hardly criticise when he preferred to live his life that way. It was easier than facing the real world where he had no one, and nowhere that felt like home.

'OK, then, let's see what we have to feed our hungry new Thaleia.' He led her towards the galley. Somewhere he didn't usually venture through fear of treading on Chef's toes, but also because he'd become accustomed to having people prepare whatever he wanted.

Thaleia popped up onto the island counter, her legs dangling, looking totally at home. She helped herself to some olives from the bowl sitting on the side. 'Just grab a few snacks. I want to chill out up top. Didn't you say something about a hot tub before?'

'Wow. You really are a different person tonight.' When he'd first suggested she join him in the tub, he'd been at his charming, flirtatious best. Mostly because he'd known she couldn't stand him and he'd enjoyed getting her riled. He'd never thought she'd actually accept the invitation at any point.

'I want to completely zone out of my life for one night. I want to live like Enzo Capelli and just have fun.' She tossed an olive at him, which he managed to catch in his mouth. He bit down, hoping the taste would take away the bitterness that had suddenly arisen.

He knew she hadn't meant it as an insult. Indeed, until recently he'd thought that was all his existence was about: having fun. However, Thaleia had been making him look at his life differently since they met, and realise there were a lot of things he needed to deal with.

That was something he'd have to analyse later. Tonight wasn't about him. It was clear Thaleia needed to let off some steam, and if there was one thing he knew how to do, it was to show people how to have a good time.

'Well, if you really want to be like me, the hot tub isn't the answer. I told you, it's my office. When I want to really let loose, I go for a swim.' He grabbed her hand, pulling her down off the counter, to follow him on deck.

She watched as he pulled off his shirt and began undoing his trousers, her eyes growing large.

'You swim in there, at night?'

He pulled off his trousers so he was standing in just his boxers. 'Yeah. Talk about freeing. It can be a little chilly, but it's safe. I don't stray too far from the yacht.'

'How do you see anything out there?'

'There's enough light from the yacht. Now, are you coming, or is the new Thaleia all talk?'

He couldn't resist a tease. Not when he knew how she would react. He liked that fiery side to her, and was glad she'd finally shown it to her parents tonight.

As predicted, Thaleia rose to the challenge. Stripping off until she stood in just her underwear. He tried not to ogle, but he was a man after all. The black satin plunge bra and high-cut panties were understated but nonetheless sexy. He was hoping the water was cool enough to take his mind, and certain other interested parts of him, off the sight of her.

'I'm ready if you are.' She came to his side with a confident stride, but he could feel her hesitation as she looked down into the dark depths of the sea below.

Enzo reached out and took her hand. 'I won't let anything happen to you, I promise.'

She bit her lip as she nodded, showing a hint of the old Thaleia who couldn't quite manage to rid herself of all her worries. It made her all the more courageous in his eyes that she was willing to do this and take another step out of her comfort zone. Perhaps once he'd moved on she might be willing to expand her own horizons too and venture beyond her shop doorway. She deserved to have a full life, with love and surrounded by people with her best interests at heart.

He knew he wasn't the one to do that for her,

who could be there for her, yet it hurt to think he wouldn't be a part of that.

'Are you ready?' he asked one last time, giving her the opportunity to say no, to make that final decision herself.

'Give me a countdown first.' Her hand tightened around his.

'On the count of three. One, two, three…' They both leapt at the same time, Thaleia's shriek filling the night air just before they hit the water.

At some point they let go of one another. Both struggling back to the surface to face one another, once the initial shock of the cold wore off.

'I should probably remind you that I'm not a great swimmer.' Thaleia slicked her hair back from her face as she treaded water. She'd waited until they'd taken the leap before voicing her fears. Likely because he might have tried to talk her out of it. Once again showing her inner strength.

'That's OK, I am. I won't let anything happen to you. We won't go too far.' Enzo rolled over onto his back and drifted, showing her this wasn't a competition. It was about chilling out and doing something just because it felt good. He was an expert in that at least, if not families and complicated emotional situations.

'OK,' she gasped through her bright smile.

He didn't think he'd ever seen her so relaxed, so happy, and he wished they could stay here for ever. Where he could protect her from anyone who might hurt her.

It occurred to him that she'd awakened a protective side in him. Something he hadn't managed at eighteen years old, when he should have been looking out for his little sister. He wasn't sure if it was a sign he'd changed, matured, or simply because he'd grown so close to Thaleia. Probably a combination. Perhaps it was time to reach out to Bea, show her he was a different person and see if they could mend their relationship. If he could overcome his fear that he'd lose her too if they got too close.

They swam, and splashed, drifted, and laughed, until Enzo's limbs were aching, and the cold began to set in.

'Why don't we warm up in the hot tub? I'll bring the snacks.' It wasn't a ploy to get her where he wanted, he was genuinely freezing his bits off now and hunger had caught up with him too.

Thaleia was shivering as he led her to the hot tub and turned on the bubbles.

'You jump in. I'll get snacks and towels.' It was nice to be in company without an agenda for once. This wasn't a seduction, it was two people unwinding after a difficult day. He was able to turn off the usual noise in his head and just be with Thaleia. There was no need to try and impress her with his money, or dazzle her with his charisma, because nothing could happen between them.

Thaleia was the first person, apart from her brother at university, who accepted him for who he was, so he didn't have to put on this front. He could relax, let his guard down tonight.

Then he walked out on the deck to see her in the hot tub, head back, eyes closed, looking serene and beautiful. He was in big trouble.

'I've got a robe for you for whenever you want to get out, and I've got olives, bread, some cold meats, and I found some dates too…' Enzo fussed around the small table nearby setting out his mezze. He seemed jittery in contrast to how content Thaleia felt right now.

Leaving her parents' party would be a small thing to most, but to her it was a big step towards her independence. To being the Thaleia who did her own thing and didn't rely on or pander to anyone. As relaxed as her body was after the midnight swim and revitalising hot tub, the rest of her was wired. Fired up from her little act of rebellion.

Was this what it felt like for Enzo on a permanent basis? Acting without fear of consequence was certainly an adrenaline sport she could get into. She was beginning to see the pros of living the way he did.

'Aren't you joining me?' She watched him with a curious eye. He'd covered his magnificently wet body in a robe and was sitting at the table popping olives into his mouth.

The Enzo she'd met on day one had done his best to get her into this hot tub and now he was acting as though it was the last place he wanted to be.

'I'm fine here. You enjoy yourself.'

He was definitely acting weird.

Deciding to join him, she stepped out and grabbed a towel to dry herself off. Aware of his eyes watching her, she took her time. She didn't know if it was her display of assertiveness in leaving the party tonight that had given her the confidence boost, but Enzo's appreciation as he looked at her was bolstering it even more. His cooling off after the kiss had been hard to take, and seeing his interest now was restoring that belief that he found her attractive after all. She found herself wanting to see more of that hungry look in his eyes.

Tonight had shown her that life was still out there to be had, to be a part of. Thanks to Enzo. It was nice just having fun, not analysing everything and simply living in the moment.

She donned the bathrobe he'd left out for her and sat in the chair next to him at the table. 'A lot has happened since we first ate here together.'

That first day she'd been so wary of him, uncomfortable around him, because he was too much like Makis. Unreliable. She'd judged him on rumour and their first meeting, and decided he was too risky to be around. Her opinion of him had entirely changed. In taking the time to get to know him, she'd seen beneath that boisterous exterior. Enzo was just as wounded by the past as she'd been, but he didn't spend his days wallowing in it, or letting it affect the rest of his life. He was living it.

OK, so he had his issues too. Hiding from the world in a different way perhaps, but he seemed to be coping better than she was on a day-to-day basis. He'd taken control of his life instead of merely letting things happen to him and reacting. It was time she did the same.

'Yeah. We managed to fake our way through a relationship twice.' Enzo took a date from one of the dishes and offered her one.

Sweet and delicious, they were easy to get addicted to. A bit like Enzo. She knew he was going to leave soon, and she was going to miss him. There were feelings there for him that could never see the light of day. She liked him, she felt comfortable with him, but he definitely wasn't the settling-down type while what she wanted was the marriage-and-children kind of relationship. It was a pity there wasn't some sort of in between. A middle ground that would let them act on the chemistry that was still bubbling away under the surface.

Even now, she could see his eyes wander to where her robe had opened, exposing her bare legs. The thought that he wanted her flooding her body with arousal. She wondered how it would feel to give into temptation. To act without thinking about how it would affect her long term. Simply having a good time. She couldn't remember the last time she'd had that before Enzo had come into her life.

'It wasn't that difficult, was it? Pretending you like me?' Her ego wanted to hear him admit that there was something between them, no matter how hard they'd tried to fight it until now.

Thaleia licked the sticky residue of the dates from her fingers, knowingly teasing him as he watched her suck her fingers. It gave her a sense of power seeing that flare of desire in his eyes, knowing he was struggling with the fight as much as she was. The difference was that she was almost ready to give in. For one night she simply wanted to feel good. Enzo couldn't hurt her when she knew there was no future to be had. He was leaving. She just wanted a goodbye to remember.

He shook his head with a grin. 'Not at all. I would've said it was you who had the harder time making peace with the idea. I could literally see the hate in your eyes that first day.'

'You grew on me.'

'I knew I'd wear you down sooner or later.'

'What gave it away? The eye rolling?' It was her way of giving attitude without saying a word. Enzo had been on the receiving end of a few of those when she'd been doing her best to push him away. Ironic when she found herself now wanting him to stick around.

'Such a turn-on.' He winked, not knowing the effect it was having on her insides.

She didn't know what was happening to her tonight. Perhaps it was the thought this could be the last time she ever saw him, but that need for him she'd tried to ignore was burning brighter than ever. What was more, she wanted to act on it.

'The kissing was kind of good too.' She leaned across the table and lifted a date to his lips.

'What are you doing, Thaleia?' He gave her a warning look but bit down on the date regardless.

She took the other half and popped it into her mouth. 'So tasty, don't you think?'

He was silent, watching for her next move. What happened now was down to her and that was an aphrodisiac in itself. Taking control of her life and acting on what she wanted for a change.

When he didn't move, didn't try to stop her, she leaned in and pressed her lips against his. That contact zapping through the rest of her body.

'I thought we agreed this was a bad idea,' he mumbled against her mouth, but made no effort to move away. As though he was waiting for confirmation that this was what she really wanted.

'Tonight has made me realise that I don't want to hide myself away, afraid to get close to anyone again.'

'Thaleia, you know I'm not husband material. I'm not even boyfriend material.'

'But you are the "love them for one night and leave them the next morning" type.'

'Usually, my bed companions are the ones to leave, but yeah, I'm a one-night-stand kind of guy. Are you telling me that's what you want?' He had his eyes fixed on her, leaving her no room for uncertainty.

She matched the intensity of his stare with her own. 'You're what I want.'

Thaleia kissed him again. This time he relaxed

against her, opening his lips to accept her, his tongue searching for hers. It wasn't long before that passion erupted between them once more. Finally released after being held in captivity for so long.

Enzo wrapped his arms around her and lifted her effortlessly so she was sitting on his lap. Bringing them closer, deepening the kiss. Her robe had fallen open and he slid his hand inside to cup her breast.

'I should get you out of these wet things before you catch cold.'

She'd forgotten she was still in her underwear until then. Now she couldn't wait for those last few scraps of fabric to fall between them. Although, as emboldened as she felt right now, on deck was not the place she wished to remove them.

'Why don't you show me your room and we can get more comfortable?' she whispered into his ear and felt him shudder.

'I think we can do that,' he growled, standing up and lifting her effortlessly with him.

He carried her down to his room, all the while Thaleia kept her arms wrapped around his neck, kissing him, and maintaining that connection. When they were finally ensconced in his room, the door closed, the romantic fantasy started to feel real.

He set her gently down onto the bed and parted her robe. *'Bellissima.'*

Thaleia shivered as he peeled away her underwear, her wet naked skin exposed to the cool air and his gaze. Enzo kissed her on the lips. A slow, thorough exploration that rendered Thaleia a puddle of arousal. Any doubts that this was a good idea melting away with every touch of his lips.

No, he wasn't her usual type, but perhaps that was what made this all the more thrilling and passionate. A one-off, never-to-be-repeated dive out of her comfort zone. Enzo was the reward for letting go, for embracing the wild side she hadn't known she had. There was nothing to say she wouldn't eventually find 'the one'. Nor did she have to forgo this kind of passion while she waited for him to come along. Enzo had shown her that those desires in her hadn't died just because her trust in men had. He'd coaxed them both back to life. It was a shame he couldn't offer her the stability she craved, or he would have been the perfect man for her.

Enzo stripped off until he was as unabashedly naked as she was. Even sexier than she'd imagined, and that was saying something. She'd had glimpses of that body, hard and taut, but that was nothing compared to the uninhibited view. For a moment she thought she was dreaming. That her imagination had willed this into being. So she reached out to touch him, her hand stroking that muscular chest, and down, down…

It was only when he gasped her name that she was convinced this was real.

Enzo took his time mapping her body with his mouth. Kissing, tasting, tonguing every inch of skin. Until she was writhing with want for more than his lips. He teased her nipple with his tongue. Softly, slowly lapping the tight tip. Thaleia felt as though she were going to combust, straining against his naked form, begging him to release this pent-up need. And when he took her nipple in his mouth, sucked hard, grazing the sensitive nub with his teeth, she cried out. It was slight relief in the face of her sudden frustration.

Her body was already slick with need, ready to accept him, but Enzo seemed determined to prolong her agony. Fingers kneading her breasts, teasing her. Lips steadily making their way down her body. Stubble tickling her belly. Then tongue lapping, darting inside her, until the pressure inside her was nearly too much to cope with. She was teetering on the brink, trying to hold back, but Enzo kept pushing. Deeper, closer to the edge. Until she fell over that cliff and into a sea of bliss.

Her orgasm tore through her whole body. Setting fireworks off in her head and rendering the rest of her body limp.

Through her dazed gaze she watched Enzo sheath his impressive erection before joining her on their bed. Joining their bodies together. A small gasp, a mixture of surprise and satisfaction, escaped her lips.

Enzo too gave a groan as he entered her, hesitating, composing himself before he moved. Thaleia wrapped her arms and legs around him, clinging to him as he drove into her. They rode the crest of their desires, until sweat glistened on their bodies and the air was filled with groans of pleasure.

And when Enzo finally reached his climax, Thaleia's delight was twofold. Not only because he brought her with him for the second time, but because she was able to help him lose control. He'd been holding back until tonight and she was glad they'd both been able to give in to their needs, even just for tonight.

Enzo collapsed down onto the bed next to her, grinning through his heavy breathing. 'Well, that was unexpected.'

'That it was good?' It was certainly more passion than she'd ever experienced. There was no mundane, scheduled sex with Enzo as a lover. It was raw, unbridled lust, from both partners. He'd awakened a side in her she hadn't known existed, and a want in her to keep exploring it. Her love life was never going to be the same again after one night with him. If she ever found another man she'd even want to share a bed with again.

He laughed. 'No, that it happened in the first place. You just keep on surprising me, Thaleia Galatis.'

'In what way?' She danced her fingers along his chest, already in the mood for a repeat performance. If they only had one night together, she was going to make the most of it.

Enzo rolled onto his side to look at her, leaning on one elbow. 'When we first met, I had you figured as this damaged, uptight loner who was happy being on her own.'

'Thanks a lot.' She couldn't say she was particularly happy with that description, probably because it was true.

'You know what I mean. You were hiding away from the world, but I've seen you blossom these past few days. Standing up against your parents, coming here tonight, making your own decisions.' He reached over to kiss her, leaving her under no illusion about what decision he was referring to.

Tonight had been her choice. They could have remained friends, with Enzo sailing off into the sunset, and her wondering what if for ever more. Instead, she'd wanted to play it dangerously. Just one night of not worrying about anyone, or anything, other than her own pleasure. Something she could have got used to if he weren't leaving. Probably what made it a good idea this could only be for one night. She didn't want to get used to needing another man who wasn't husband material. That was a road right to heartbreak.

'You've changed too, you know.' It was evident his conscience was bothered about how he'd left things with Alex and Bea, and she thought it important for him to know that he was a good man. She thought so, regardless that he tried to convince himself otherwise.

'Oh, I know. I never believed I'd be playing the doting boyfriend at the parents' anniversary party.'

'That's not what I meant. Although I appreciate you stepping out of character for me.' Because she'd come to see that was who 'Bacchus' was behind that nickname. The drinking and partying, the endless parade of girls he must have had through here, were all a cover so he didn't have to deal with his past.

She didn't want to dwell too long on the thought of him sharing this bed with other women. Though she contented herself that those bed partners had spent the night with 'Bacchus'. As far as she knew she was the only one to sleep with the real Enzo.

'So what did you mean?'

'When we first met you were cocky and self-centred. Annoying. A caricature. Bacchus brought to life.'

'Don't hold back, will you?' The frown marring his forehead told her he was a little wounded by her assessment, but she wanted him to know she saw the real him behind the mask.

She stroked his forehead until the frown went away. 'I'm saying that's not the real you. Enzo Capelli is kind and considerate—'

'And an incredible lover,' he finished for her.

'Of course.' She had no doubt 'Bacchus' was good in bed too, but it had felt more than just sex with Enzo. On her part, she knew she'd been expressing her growing feelings for him. She didn't dare wish it were the same for him.

'Just do me one favour.'

'Name it.' Thaleia laid her head on his chest, looking up at him while her hand slid under the sheets.

'Don't mention this to your brother.'

Thaleia knew he was only half joking, which was what saved him from serious injury. 'Trust me, my brother is the last person I would tell about this.'

She didn't know why he had such a bee in his bonnet about Alex, but she didn't want to get into it. There was no need when this was a one-off, and she didn't want to spoil it by talking about her brother. Besides, she doubted she'd get to gossip about this with anyone. She'd left her whole life behind when she'd moved here. The only person on the island she could confide in was Agathi, and Thaleia thought the old woman knew this was going to happen before they did.

'So, tomorrow, when we're back in Paxos, you're just going back to your life working in the shop, and I'm going to sail away like this never happened.' Enzo tackled the subject she was hoping they could avoid until tomorrow, but he burst the bubble. Reminding her that this was only a temporary state of happiness.

'That's the plan. Just one night having fun, and back to real life.' For her at least. Enzo would likely carry on with this same scenario night after night with a different woman.

'Then I guess we should make it one to remember.' Enzo rolled her over onto her back and she let out a cry of surprise.

He was kissing her again. Dragging her back into the fantasy, and she didn't resist. This was where she wanted to be tonight. Tomorrow would come soon enough, and she wasn't in any hurry to go back to being Thaleia Galatis, jilted bride, lonely jewellery maker.

CHAPTER ELEVEN

Enzo had watched the crew getting the yacht ready for its onward journey without the usual fizzing in his veins, ready for the next chapter. He found himself reluctant to leave this one unfinished. They'd sailed to Paxos overnight, and Thaleia had gone ashore early this morning. Leaving last night as an enjoyable, erotic memory. With no promises about the future.

For the first time in recent history he hadn't brought a woman on board with the intent to sleep with her, but it had happened anyway. Thaleia had wanted to spend the night with him, and her confident insistencc had been all it took for his resolve to crumble away.

'So, where are we off to today, sir?' The captain came to him in his study, quite rightly wanting to know what the plan was.

Enzo didn't usually leave it until this late to decide his next destination, but a lot of things were different these days. He'd already stayed longer than he would do in one place and that was entirely down to Thaleia. His usual wanderlust that drove him had morphed more into lust, and perhaps even something else.

'I'm not sure… I might hold off until the end of the day to make that decision. Sorry.' Enzo knew once they hauled anchor out of here he might never see Thaleia again and he didn't think he was ready for that. Especially after last night.

Sleeping with her last night hadn't been just sex. It had hit differently. Not only was his body sated, but he'd felt a peace being with her. Until dawn had broken and she'd gone home, and he'd realised his emotions were all over the place. Normally this was the point where he ran. He didn't get close to his bedfellows, but he and Thaleia had bonded long before they'd given into temptation.

The way he led his life meant it was uncomplicated, but Thaleia had made it anything but. A one-time deal was ordinarily fine with him, but this was different. Making love to Thaleia last night, and the early hours of the morning, was something he could get used to on a regular basis.

That should have been enough to send him sailing at high speed across the ocean. He liked Thaleia. She made him want to stick around. A red flag for anyone who had a problem with commitment and dealing with emotions. Something he'd been running from for over a decade, and he knew being with Thaleia meant facing those.

As well as Enzo not wanting to hurt Alex, or his little sister, she had her own personal demons to deal with. A woman who wanted a husband and family, who'd already been jilted at the altar, wouldn't enter into any sort of relationship lightly. Enzo didn't want to hurt her, yet he wasn't sure he could give her everything she needed in a partner either. It was a quandary he'd never thought he'd have to face, yet he couldn't find the strength to leave. Not now when he might have the chance to be content. To quieten the noise in his head without having to surround himself with strangers and loud music.

The only way he could make that decision, to stay or go, was by spending more time with Thaleia. If she wanted him to. He hadn't forgotten the pact he'd made with Alex, but he'd come to the realisation that being with Thaleia was worth risking his best friend's wrath.

'I think you are in another place today.' Agathi tutted as she left a pastry beside Thaleia's work station.

'I didn't hear you come in. Sorry.' Her mind had definitely been in another place. It was difficult to concentrate on cutting sheets of silver when all she could think of was being in Enzo's bed last night.

It had been incredible. She'd never felt so alive, so much like herself. Free from her parents' control, the pain of the past and, probably, common sense. If she'd thought one night with him would be enough, would stop this yearning, she'd been wrong. And to what end? He was leaving, if he hadn't left already.

The thought of never seeing him again was painful. Yet she didn't think their time together had meant as much to him as it had to her. He hadn't bothered to come with her this morning. To say a proper goodbye. Even breakfast together had been a quiet, flirt-free affair. Either he couldn't wait to get rid of her, or he was regretting sleeping with her. It was difficult to tell which when he wouldn't open up to her.

Perhaps she'd fallen for 'Bacchus' instead of Enzo after all, since once he'd got what he wanted, he was apparently done with her.

Agathi took Thaleia's face in her hands and turned her around. 'You are glowing. I see it. I know a woman in love.'

'No. That's not...you're wrong...' Thaleia turned away so Agathi wouldn't see the confusion written all over her face. The truth was, she didn't know what to feel.

Last night had been about taking control, and now it seemed as though everything was spiralling away from her. Enzo was leaving, and all she knew was that she didn't want him to. There was unfinished business, or else why would she be in such turmoil about him going?

If it had been just sex, a way to relieve the tension between them, she should be more than satisfied. Except she wasn't. There was an even greater void inside her knowing that he'd gone from her life.

Perhaps last night had been more about her feelings towards him than she'd cared to admit, and she'd only made things worse by sleeping with him. Knowing what they could be like together, when there was no chance of that happening on a long-term basis. Her own fault, of course. On that subject he'd been more than honest about his aversion to commitment. She hadn't asked for or expected more than one night, but it hurt that he hadn't wanted more after all.

Wounded pride more than wounded heart, she tried to tell herself.

'Uh-huh.' Agathi's non-believing tone was worse than her arguing.

Enzo chose that moment to stroll in nonchalantly, and Thaleia had to put her game face on in case either of them saw her delight.

'I, er, wasn't expecting to see you today.' Or ever again.

'I'll be on my way. People to see.' Agathi pushed past her but didn't leave without a knowing glance between Thaleia and Enzo.

'OK. Thanks, Agathi,' Thaleia called after her, trying to sound normal.

'Hi. Bye.' Enzo nodded at Agathi as she rushed out of the door, leaving them alone.

'I thought you'd be gone by now.' Thaleia swallowed hard as he walked towards her, looking as gorgeous as ever. Though she preferred the ruffled, naked, just-had-sex version she'd woken up beside this morning.

That had been the revelation to her, as much as the sex. She'd done her best to convince herself she was content here on the island by herself. Yet she hadn't wanted to leave his embrace, or his bed. It was the nicest feeling in the world to be held close, to hear his heart beating rhythmically as she lay on his chest. Protected. Loved. Feelings she hadn't experienced in a long time. It had made her consider the idea of a relationship again and how much she'd like to have those things on a permanent basis. Enzo had taught her how to trust again, to open her life to someone else. The problem being that someone else was completely unavailable to her.

'So did I.' He walked towards her with purpose, kicking her heart rate up a notch until he was right in front of her. Then he kissed her and she was sure she was about to go into cardiac arrest.

As welcome and lovely as the kiss was, soft and tender, and turning her to liquid, her brain wouldn't switch off and simply let her enjoy it. She needed to know why. Why he was still here, and why he was kissing her. What it meant. Her emotions were in enough of a tangle and she didn't want to add this into the mix until she had an explanation.

'Why are you here, Enzo?' she asked.

'I thought you'd be pleased to see me.' He cocked his head to one side and gave her big puppy-dog eyes, which couldn't fail to make her smile.

'You know I am.' There was little point hiding that from him when it had been evident last night how much she enjoyed being with him. She simply wanted to know what had happened in between her leaving this morning and now for him to even consider staying.

It wouldn't be good for her heart to get her hopes up prematurely.

'When the captain asked for the new route I simply couldn't bring myself to leave the island. At least not yet.'

'Why not?' Thaleia swallowed down the excitement rising in her chest. If he was willing to give them a chance as a couple, make some sort of commitment, it meant she didn't have to keep her guard up any more. She could let him in farther than the bedroom door.

Though she was afraid to believe that he could be the perfect package in case he let her down. It seemed too much of a fairy tale to have a handsome, kind, excellent lover who wanted to be with her. The last time she'd believed in her happy ever after she had been brought back down to earth with a soul-crushing thump.

Enzo stood back, giving them both some breathing room. 'To be honest, I don't know. You. Me. What might be possible. This is new territory for me and I don't want to make a promise I can't keep, but I would like to stay a while longer. Spend more time with you and see what happens.'

It wasn't a real commitment, but rather a tentative exploration. Thaleia wished she were strong enough to say no, that it wasn't enough for her to feel safe, but she was willing to take the small crumb he was offering. The chance to be with him for a little longer, but without the safety of a proper relationship that she needed.

'What does that mean? A fling? A casual thing? Friends with benefits?' She needed clarification so she could adjust her feelings accordingly. If he wasn't prepared to commit wholly, then neither could she. It was self-preservation to keep a part of her heart closed at least. Then when the time inevitably came when he'd leave, she wouldn't be completely broken-hearted.

Enzo leaned back against her work bench and folded his arms. 'Do we have to put a label on it? Can't we just go with the flow?'

That smile of his was seriously disarming, but his words put the tension back in her body. This was his get-out clause. If he couldn't handle being with the same woman for too long, he'd bolt. With a clear conscience. After all, he wasn't promising her a relationship. He was keeping his options open. It was down to Thaleia whether or not she wanted to agree to those terms.

'What changed your mind? I got the impression you couldn't wait to get rid of me this morning.' She couldn't keep the hurt from her voice, nor stop the defiant tilt of her chin. Challenging him to tell her the truth. If she was simply a stopgap until he got bored she'd rather know now before her feelings for him developed any further.

'That's not true. I was doing my best to stick to the plan. One night only, we agreed. Except I realised I wanted more so I panicked. That was my cue to get out of here. So I pushed you away, ready to run. But I couldn't go.' He reached out and stroked her cheek.

Despite all the warnings her inner jilted bride was shouting at her, Thaleia leaned into his touch. Wanting it. Needing it. Her heart overruling her head again.

'Don't hurt me, Enzo.' She hadn't meant to say it, and the words came out so softly she wasn't one hundred per cent sure she had until Enzo gathered her into a hug.

'I don't want to. This is a big step for me too. But if you don't want to take a chance on me, on us, I'll understand.' He was leaving the decision down to her. A huge leap of faith in someone she already knew was completely wrong for her.

Perhaps that was where she'd been going wrong. Trying to force the person she wanted to be with into the mould of the man she needed. Her ex obviously hadn't wanted marriage, at least not with her. It was possible she'd railroaded him into that idea because she'd thought it was the only thing that would make her happy. Enzo was the opposite of that perfect husband and father she thought she needed in her life, but these days with him had been when she'd felt most content. Moving to the island was supposed to be the start of her new life, and maybe that meant changing her outlook on her love life.

She'd thought a husband and a family of her own would make her complete somehow. That it was the only way to have love in her life when her parents had denied it to her growing up. A longing that had managed to cloud her judgement over Makis.

This time with Enzo had nearly been enough, just knowing someone cared about her. How much could it hurt simply to have that in her life a little longer?

She thought back to last night when she'd been afraid to jump off the yacht into the water. When Enzo had taken her hand and made her believe she could do anything because he'd be there with her.

'I'm ready if you are,' she said, hoping it was true. That she was ready to enter into something that wasn't guaranteed. She was putting her faith in Enzo, and herself, that, whatever happened, she wouldn't live to regret acting on impulse for once.

CHAPTER TWELVE

'WHEN YOU SAID you were going to show me the sights, I didn't think that meant I'd be hiking.' Enzo dumped his rucksack onto the ground, took out a bottle of water and poured it over his head before taking a drink.

'No, you probably expected an air-conditioned ride in a limo. This is getting back to nature. It's good for you.' Thaleia kissed him on the cheek and took the bottle of water from him.

She took a swig of water while admiring the surroundings. This was a leafier area of the island, but more humid. It had been thirsty work getting here but she was sure it was worth it. This past couple of weeks with Enzo had been lovely. He gave her space to carry on with her work, and in the afternoons they ventured out for walks, most times taking a picnic as they had that first time on the beach.

At night they slept together. Sometimes on the yacht, but more often at her place. Enzo seemed to be getting more and more comfortable with the idea of staying in one place, and she had to admit she was getting used to their routine. She was content, happy and didn't want things to end.

'How much further?' Enzo was doubled over, doing his best to get his breath back.

'Not far. Come on. There will be more shade there.' It had been hotter than she'd anticipated today, making the trek a little more arduous than normal, and she was feeling it too. Still, it would be worth the pay-off at the end. It was a beautiful spot. Somewhere Enzo wouldn't have seen from the deck of his yacht. He was missing so much by living out there on the ocean, never venturing too far from his safe place. Until this week. Thaleia was hoping she was showing him there was nothing to fear. They were both breaking their own rules and, so far, the world hadn't ended.

'There'd better be,' Enzo grumbled. 'We could be sitting on deck drinking cocktails, you know.'

'I would've thought you'd be getting tired of that,' she teased, grabbing his hand and pulling him onward.

Enzo groaned, and grabbed his rucksack, hoisting it onto his shoulders again. 'Strangely not. This better be worth it, *cara mia*.'

With a renewed burst of energy, Enzo lunged at her from behind, catching her around the waist. Making her squeal as he kissed her neck enthusiastically. Thaleia spun around and draped her arms around his neck. Kissing him back in that long lazy way she enjoyed so much. When the world felt as though it were theirs and they had all the time in the world together.

Except the sudden spinning in her head cut the leisurely embrace short. She extracted herself from Enzo and, bent over, hands on her thighs, she took deep breaths.

'Hey, are you OK?' Her suddenly concerned hiking companion came to her at once.

'I just felt dizzy all of a sudden.'

'Let's get you sat down somewhere.' Enzo unhooked her backpack to carry it himself.

'It's not too far to the top. There's a bench to sit on there.' It wasn't exactly why she'd brought him all this way, but the end game was all the same.

With Enzo keeping a tight hold of her, they made their way up the incline to the seat.

'This is why you brought me all the way up here?' He wasn't too impressed until she turned his face around so he could see the view over the entire island. Including her shop perched on the cliff, and his yacht in the distance.

'Wow.'

'See. I told you it was worth it.' Although, as she sipped at the lukewarm water, the sun beating down on them, she was beginning to doubt herself.

'It is a fantastic view, but I'm more concerned with you right now. How are you feeling?'

'Dizzy. Nauseated.' She was fighting against the sudden swirling in her stomach, determined not to be sick and spoil this moment.

Things had been so good between them she'd been thinking about asking him to make more of a commitment. To see if he wanted to move in with her. Yes, it was a risk, but she was sure it was time to take the next step and she wanted it to be with Enzo.

'Could be the heat,' he suggested, nudging the water bottle and coaxing her to take another drink.

'I'd been feeling fine until we stopped.' Although it was warm, she hadn't been struggling with the heat or the exercise.

'Maybe it's low blood sugar. Have you eaten today?'

'Yes. You made breakfast, remember?' In fact he'd brought her breakfast in bed before climbing back in beside her.

'Of course.' Enzo smacked his forehead. 'How could I have forgotten?'

'We were a bit preoccupied…' she reminded him, since they'd got caught up with other activities soon after.

A grin spread over his features. 'Oh, yeah. That happens a lot.'

They were still very much in the honeymoon phase and took every opportunity they could to be intimate.

Wait…

A sudden fear gripped Thaleia. Her period was late. There was that sick feeling again in the pit of her stomach.

'What? What is it?' Enzo, who'd been watching her very carefully, had apparently seen the panic play out over her features.

It would probably be better for her to get back and take a pregnancy test before she freaked him out, but it was a long walk back and she wouldn't be able to avoid his questioning for ever. A pregnancy was the last thing either of them had planned on, or wanted, but it was one possible reason for her sudden nausea.

'I've just realised I'm late.'

It took a moment for him to register what she was talking about. The colour draining from his face when the penny dropped. 'Late, late?'

She nodded.

'That's impossible. I'm always so careful.' He was holding his head in his hands as though his world had just ended.

Enzo was usually careful when it came to contraception, but pregnancy wasn't a completely off-the-wall idea.

'Apart from that first night on the yacht.' They'd used a condom the first time they'd slept together, but passion had taken over from common sense at some point during the night, if she recalled correctly.

Enzo swore and Thaleia's heart dropped into her stomach. The happy-go-lucky, charming Enzo had disappeared. Replaced by a stern-looking stranger. 'How could I have been so stupid?'

'It takes two to do what we did.' She attempted to lighten the mood but only succeeded in furrowing his brow further.

'I can't be a father. I couldn't even be a big brother.' He was spiralling, and she understood why, but it wasn't going to help the situation.

'It might not even be that. It could be heatstroke. We won't know until we get back and do a test.' She was trying to convince herself as much as Enzo that things would be all right. Yet she couldn't help but think what it would be like to have Enzo's baby.

It wouldn't be the end of the world as far as she was concerned. She could easily imagine being a mother. Once upon a time that was all she'd wanted. However, it was clear from his dark expression that he didn't feel the same. Their time together these past weeks had lulled her into a false sense of security, believing he was making a commitment to her. Perhaps this was a commitment too far.

'We should get back.' Enzo got to his feet, lifting both of their bags, waiting for her to move. So much for their lovely romantic afternoon.

Enzo was doing his best not to freak out and shove his head in the sand the way he had when he'd been left to look after Beatrice. At least not until they knew for sure what they were dealing with.

Though he knew Thaleia wasn't trying to trap him into a lifetime commitment, he felt trapped all the same. They were barely a couple so what chance did they have to make this work? To be a family? When he'd failed in running the family business and maintaining a relationship with his sister after his parents had died. A few days with someone he cared about couldn't possibly change his whole personality so that he was suddenly an emotionally adjusted adult capable of being a good father.

It wasn't Thaleia's fault he'd been so stupid. He should've been more careful not to end up in this position. Instead, he'd let his libido take control and potentially ruined three lives. Because he could never be the man Thaleia and a baby needed.

He'd fallen for her and let his feelings impair his judgement. The very reason he should never have stayed in the first place. He'd taken one step out of his safe place and now he was being whisked into a new realm where he'd no desire to be.

They'd made their way back to Thaleia's house almost in silence. He knew she was upset, probably frightened too, but so was he. This wasn't in the plan. All he'd wanted was a sense of normality for once. Being able to be with someone without feeling the need to run. Except now he was stuck. Responsible for whatever had happened, and whatever happened next. Everything he'd been trying to avoid since he was eighteen.

'I can run to the store and get you a pregnancy test. You stay here and rest,' Enzo called through the bathroom door. Thaleia had gone in to freshen up as soon as they'd arrived.

She didn't answer, but opened the door to face him. 'False alarm. I guess I was just late after all. That's probably why I was feeling out of sorts. Sorry for the panic.'

Relief knocked Enzo off his feet and onto the sofa. 'You're sure?'

'I'm definitely not pregnant. We can relax.' Thaleia hovered in the doorway, still looking more upset than relieved.

For a moment he'd thought about Thaleia as

the mother of his child. She'd have made a perfect mother. It didn't seem fair that she was with someone who was terrified at the prospect of having a baby. His worst nightmare.

This had been a lucky escape for him, and he never wanted to come this close again. It was a sign he'd let his guard down too far, too fast. He'd only known Thaleia a number of weeks and they'd already had a pregnancy scare. If he stuck around much longer there was a danger he'd end up trapped in a relationship he'd never wanted. He was definitely the wrong man for someone who hadn't seemed too perturbed at the thought of an unplanned pregnancy. It was a disaster waiting to happen for both of them.

'I'm not sure I can, Thaleia.' Even as he said it, he felt ill. He didn't want to do this to her, or himself, but he'd stayed too long. Taken one too many chances, and he couldn't afford to slip up in any way. This wasn't just his heart on the line, it was Thaleia's, and he would never forgive himself if he hurt her.

'What are you saying, Enzo?' She tilted her chin up, her blazing eyes demanding he say it so there was no confusion.

'I've been here before. The last time I was responsible for a child, I left her to go partying. I know the circumstances aren't the same, and you're not pregnant, but we both know I'm not the man you, or your future child, need. I honestly think you'd be better off without me, Thaleia. Then you might have a chance of finding someone who wants to settle down as much as you do.'

His feelings for Thaleia were stronger than ever, but that was what worried him. He didn't want to be responsible for her happiness when he couldn't guarantee it. She deserved, and needed, someone better than him in her life. Someone who could give her everything she wanted. A husband. A family. That man could never be him and there was little point staying, prolonging the inevitable, and making it worse for both of them.

'We're over?' Thaleia's question almost sounded like a statement of acceptance.

'We're over,' he confirmed. Saying the words felt as though a piece of him were dying. Likely the piece of his heart that already belonged to Thaleia.

Eyes closed, she took a deep breath and eventually said, 'If that's what you want.'

She was making it easier for him to walk away. More than he deserved.

'You're a wonderful woman, Thaleia. I'm sure you'll meet someone else.' He almost cringed, hearing how patronising it sounded, even though he meant it. She would make someone a wonderful wife. It just wouldn't be him.

He opened the door and walked away. Thaleia didn't follow. They didn't even say goodbye. He was leaving the woman who'd captured his heart behind for ever, because that was the only way he could survive.

Thaleia watched him go. Stared at the closed door wondering what the hell had just happened. Only this morning he'd brought her breakfast in bed, they'd made love and gone for a romantic afternoon stroll. Now he was gone.

All because of a short-lived pregnancy scare and a garbled excuse about not being a good enough father for her future children. Whatever his reasons, he couldn't get away quick enough from the idea that he might be expected to make a commitment of some sort. Regardless that she hadn't asked anything of him.

She'd thought they had more than that between them. That he wanted to be with her, or else he wouldn't have broken his own rules in the first place. Yet he'd proved at the first hurdle they'd faced that she couldn't rely on him. He couldn't wait to be absolved of responsibility so he could leave.

It seemed he was just another playboy after all, with no intention of ever putting anyone else's needs before his own. It was her fault she felt so let down for expecting more from him.

He'd never promised her anything, but it didn't make losing him any less painful.

Thaleia moved to the door, her legs unsteady beneath her. She locked the door and turned the closed sign over, wishing she could do the same with her heart. That it was as easy to simply close him out and never think about him again, or the life she'd begun to see them building together.

She leaned her head on the door and cried until her throat and her heart were sore.

CHAPTER THIRTEEN

'IT'S FROM MY own vineyard.' Enzo poured wine for all the guests he'd invited on board.

He'd met them in a club ashore Corfu and brought everyone back for a party at his. The wine, and investment in a long-forgotten vineyard, had been his knee-jerk reaction to losing Thaleia from his life two weeks ago. Or rather, pushing her out of his life. He'd needed something to occupy his thoughts, to keep him too busy to dwell on his loss. It hadn't worked.

The whole time he'd been sampling the product and making the deal, he'd been thinking about Thaleia. Wondering what she was doing, and if she'd be pleased by the choices he was making now. It was at her suggestion that he should find something better to fill his days than women and alcohol.

The problem was, he had, and he'd thrown it away. His mind and body had never been more content than those weeks he'd spent with her on the island. No longer running from the thought of a relationship. Almost embracing it. A normal life with a wonderful woman. He was beginning to wonder what was so wrong with that. Especially when he'd been feeling so miserable since he'd left. Barely getting through the days. As though he were functioning with only half his heart and soul in operation. Despite everything he had in his life, it wasn't what he wanted. None of it was making him happy. Because all he wanted was to be with Thaleia.

'Aren't you getting in with us, Enzo?' The curvaceous blonde he'd escorted personally onto the yacht was lounging in the hot tub with a few of her friends, fluttering fake eyelashes at him. Normally he'd dive-bomb right in there, but none of it interested him any more. This past couple of weeks he'd tried his best to put Thaleia out of mind by filling his time with beautiful strangers, but it hadn't worked. He couldn't bring himself to be with any of them.

Perhaps it was the thought of Thaleia witnessing the scene. Rolling her eyes at him as if to tell him how tragic this all was in an effort to avoid his feelings. Maybe imaginary Thaleia was right. He'd done his best to fill his life with people and distractions, noise to drown out what his heart was trying to tell him. That he missed her. That he'd lost the best thing to ever happen to him. There was only one woman he had any interest in.

'Maybe later.' He passed the glasses of wine out to the revellers, sensing he'd become more the host than one of the party people.

One look around his yacht told him that this wasn't where he wanted to be. Young people grinding on each other, drinking, lounging in his hot tub. Usually he'd be in amongst it, the music and fun cranked up to a hundred, but he might as well have been here on his own. He didn't feel part of it. He didn't want it.

Making sure he'd left enough booze and food out for his guests, he took himself off to his study. It wouldn't be good for his reputation if he simply turned off the music and told everyone to go home. Taking himself out of the picture was easier than dealing with the fallout.

He gave a bitter laugh. That was true for his whole life. It was exactly what he'd done when he'd been left with Bea, and when he'd found himself falling for Thaleia. He'd removed himself from the scene so he didn't have to confront his emotions. It was easier to stay away and pretend none of it was happening. Not be around for the responsibility of caring for another person, because he didn't think he was up to the job. Never having to face his grief, his responsibility or the love he felt for anyone in his life.

He'd avoided it since losing his parents. A loss he'd probably never dealt with properly because it was so overwhelming. Instead, Enzo had been dodging getting close to anyone so it would never happen again. Then Thaleia had come along. He supposed she would have said it was he who'd burst into her life. Either way, meeting her, getting to know her, falling for her, had upended his too.

Suddenly he'd begun to see what was important, real, and it wasn't strangers taking advantage of his hospitality. He'd found more joy in the simple things like picnics and walks, and connecting with someone on more than a physical level, than he'd ever found in his hedonistic lifestyle.

Enzo grabbed a book from his library and sat down, hoping he could find something else to capture his attention other than his foolishness in falling back into old habits instead of embracing the potential of a different future. One with someone he cared about rather than a yacht full of strangers he didn't know. Too late, he was realising he wanted a relationship with Thaleia. The thought of having a baby, a lifelong commitment, had simply been too much, and he'd reverted to type. But he wasn't happy here, even in the lap of luxury. He lacked for nothing, except for the one thing that truly made him happy. Thaleia.

If having a family was what she wanted, what it took to have her in his life, he should have been willing to at least try. To make an effort to work through his issues if it meant being together. Instead, he'd run away rather than face up to his feelings for her.

Enzo tossed the unread book aside with a sigh, deciding he might as well go to bed and try to sleep. Tomorrow, he could move someplace else and try to do it all over again, hoping for a different outcome. That he'd find something, someone who could make him feel the way Thaleia had, if even for a short time.

'So this is where you're hiding.' The study door burst open and his blonde friend staggered over, spilling wine from the glass in her hand.

He forced a smile. 'I must be getting old. I needed a time-out.'

'Never. You'll be young at heart for ever, Enzo.' Her words weren't as comforting as she'd likely imagined.

Did he really still want to be doing this when he was old enough to be a father, or even grandfather, to these young clubbers he brought on board? To some men the answer might have been a resounding yes, but he'd seen a glimpse at another life, and he had a feeling he wanted that more.

Before he could get another word out, the young woman had jumped onto his lap, putting her glass to his lips and making him drink.

'I'm not really feeling it tonight,' he said, trying to get her to take a hint, but she wouldn't be deterred.

'Let me help you.' She began kissing his neck and along his jaw.

Enzo tried to force himself to enjoy it, to let go, then maybe Thaleia would be erased altogether. Except he didn't want this stranger to kiss him, to touch him where Thaleia had. It felt like a betrayal to both of them. Everything inside him was rejecting the notion of anyone touching him the way Thaleia had, because she was the only person he wanted to be intimate with.

Despite everything in his head telling him that this was who he was and he should embrace it, his heart was telling him it was wrong. He was no longer 'Bacchus'. He was Enzo Capelli, and his heart belonged to Thaleia Galatis.

He stood up, taking the girl with him and setting her feet first onto the floor. 'Sorry. It's not going to happen.'

There hadn't been the slightest stirring for a bikini-clad bombshell sitting on his lap, nibbling his ear. Thaleia had ruined him for any other woman. Enzo was in love and, no matter how terrifying it was to admit it and leave himself vulnerable to rejection, for once he was going to confront his feelings head-on. Even if that meant coming clean to Alex about breaking the pact too.

Whatever happened between him and Thaleia, Enzo had to at least tell her how he felt and see if she would even give him a second chance to be with her.

He didn't want anyone else, but he knew it would take something special to convince Thaleia he wasn't going to run again. Enzo was determined to do whatever it took to be the man she deserved.

'Your work is stunning.' A customer in the shop was turning over the brooch Thaleia had lovingly crafted in her hand.

'Thanks. I take inspiration from my surroundings.' In this case, the silver yacht finished with turquoise and blue enamelling had been her love letter to Enzo.

She should have hated him for not being the man she wanted, or who she hoped he could be, but she didn't. Only love could hurt this much. So she'd channelled the pain and loneliness she felt since he'd gone into her work. Into the ruby-encrusted heart drop earrings, and the bottle-of-champagne pendant with diamond bubbles.

Everything she'd created lately had been a homage to the relationship they'd never had.

Even the series of baby-inspired charms she'd created. A bottle, a pram, building blocks and a stork…all things to celebrate the birth of a new life. She'd never been pregnant, but for that brief moment when it had seemed a possibility, she'd seen a life with Enzo and their child. A family.

A stupid romantic fantasy when the husband in the idyll was a known commitment-phobe. Though it hadn't stopped the longing. She didn't know where she went from here when the man she wanted it all with wasn't available. So she'd simply thrown herself back into her work.

'Hello…' The tourist, who'd told Thaleia she was on a cruise stop, was standing at the cash desk staring at her, brooch in hand.

'Sorry. I was miles away. Did you say something?' Thaleia plastered on her customer-friendly smile. The one she deployed to try and get sales, regardless that smiling was the last thing she felt like doing.

'I said, I'll take this, please.' The customer handed it over for Thaleia to box up.

'No problem.' She took her time gift-wrapping the yacht, almost reluctant to let it go. It represented Enzo, and the days following his abrupt departure.

He'd disappeared the morning after the pregnancy scare, leaving her to cry over the loss. This piece literally had her tears in its very fabric.

The woman tapped her contactless card in payment, and Thaleia was forced to say goodbye. It was business, and that was all she had now.

'Enjoy the rest of your trip.' Thaleia handed over the precious reminder of Enzo with a bright smile, wondering how she was ever going to move on. She'd fallen in love with him the moment he'd tried to be someone he wasn't for her. For two weeks he'd played the part of a devoted partner, and she'd believed in the fairy tale. Imagined that they could have had it for real. That was what had made it all so difficult when Enzo had left, and proved she'd had him all wrong. Confirmed that she'd made the same mistake again, falling for someone who didn't want her after all.

Once she'd waved her customer off, Thaleia walked over to the door to close it behind her. She was done for the day. As she pushed it shut, a force from the other side pushed it open.

'Excuse me?' She stumbled back, and when she saw who it was forcing his way into the shop, she had to hold onto the nearby display case to steady herself.

Enzo.

'Hi,' he said softly, giving her a look so intense that it melted her bones and made her heart skip a beat.

'What—what are you doing here?' Her befuddled brain couldn't conjure up any logical reason why he should be here in her shop now, two weeks after he'd walked out of it without a backward glance.

'I missed you.' A simple, straight-to-the-point answer, but it didn't begin to explain why he'd come back, or what he wanted from her.

As much as Thaleia had longed to have him back in her life, she couldn't go through this again.

'What do you want?' She wasn't going to give him the satisfaction of admitting she'd missed him. If he was after another fling, he'd come to the wrong woman. It might have felt good at the time, but the heartache had proved too much in the end. She might have convinced herself once that she was the kind of woman who could pick up and drop a man when the mood took her, but it had been a lie. Her heart wanted what it wanted, and nothing less than a commitment would get her to open it up to anyone else again.

'You.' He moved towards her, but she backed away before he could touch her and make her forget why she had to keep her distance from him.

'No. I can't do this again.'

'I'm sorry, Thaleia. I really am.'

'You just left me.' She hated the teary sound of her voice as she recalled the devastating moment he'd walked out on her, but she couldn't pretend to him any more about who she was. She wasn't one of his casual girlfriends who was at his disposal any time he sailed into port.

'I know. You have no idea how much I regret acting the way I did. It's just—'

'The idea of being tied to me, to a baby, was too much. I understand.' She did. He'd always been honest about that. It was Thaleia who hadn't been honest with herself about the strength of her feelings for him. Who had convinced herself that one night, then a casual relationship, would be enough for her. Deep down she'd always been hoping for more. That was on her, not him. She'd learned from an ex that she couldn't change a man.

'Yes, but I should have stayed. I could have reacted differently. I'm sorry.'

'It doesn't change things, though, does it? We're too different, Enzo. We want different things. If you came back to ask for forgiveness, you're forgiven. If you want something more than that, then I'm sorry too, but that ship sailed away with you.' Taking a piece of her heart with him that she could never get back. She would never feel complete again.

'I came back for you, Thaleia. I thought you'd be better off without me. But I miss you. I miss us.'

'There is no us, Enzo. There never was. Not really. Whether it was playing make believe on your yacht, or playing house here, it wasn't real.' Not when she hadn't been honest with him, or herself, about her feelings for him. That likely would have sent him running earlier.

'I'm done with pretending, Thaleia. My old life holds nothing I want any more. I want to be with you, whatever that means. I'll sell my yacht, buy a place on the island, move in here, whatever it takes to make you believe I'm serious.' The sincerity was there in his eyes, in the pleading to get her to believe him. And she did.

'I can't, Enzo. I've been hurt too many times. What if you get cold feet again? I don't want to put myself through this again.' Her heart wanted him, there was no denying it, but that fragile part of her that was left was afraid he'd shatter her altogether with another rejection.

Enzo sighed, running his hands through his hair, as though he was searching for the right words to convince her this was a good idea. 'I've realised that what you said about me was true. I've been running away from real life for years. Avoiding relationships and commitment so I didn't have to deal with my feelings. Thinking that if I kept emotions out of everything, I never had to feel overwhelmed and guilty about not being enough for anyone again the way I did after my parents died. The way I felt I let Beatrice down.'

'You did your best, making sure Beatrice was safe and happy, and you visited when you could. OK, in hindsight, you feel you could have done more, and you may have drifted apart, but it's not too late to fix things. I know if Alex were to reach out, I'd be over the moon.'

It was clear Enzo was still beating himself up over that particular relationship and he wanted to do better. She hoped the same was true where she was concerned too.

'I want to patch things up with Bea, but I also wanted to tell you how I feel about you. I love you, Thaleia, and there's no running from that. Not any more. I promise I'll never hurt you again, Thaleia. I don't want anyone else. I just want you. Us.'

He walked towards her, arms outstretched, offering her the chance of a future together with him. She believed he was willing to give up everything for her, not that she wanted him to. The thought that he would do that was enough for her. If he was willing to sacrifice his old life, and the hang-ups that had kept them apart, then she had to do the same if they were ever going to stand a chance.

'So do I,' Thaleia said, walking into his arms. Embracing the man she knew she loved, and hopefully the future she'd always wanted.

EPILOGUE

One Month Later

'You may now kiss the bride.' The celebrant smiled as he gave them permission to seal their marriage with a kiss.

Enzo was wearing his white cotton shirt and linen trousers, and Thaleia had donned the summer dress embellished with lemons that she'd worn on their first picnic. They were both barefoot as they said their vows on the very beach they'd visited that day. Agathi and her widowed friend had stood as witnesses. A quiet, private ceremony that neither Enzo nor Thaleia had told anyone else about. Deciding that they didn't want their special day spoiled by family politics or bad feeling when both of their families had been fractured long before they'd got together.

The fact that they were together was likely to ruffle a few feathers anyway, especially with her brother. Though they were hoping to reconcile everyone with the idea that they were now a married couple by throwing a party at a later date to celebrate their nuptials. Enzo particularly wanted to mend his relationship with Beatrice and planned to have a heart-to-heart conversation with her at some point to explain how he'd felt after their parents' deaths, and why he'd acted the way he had.

Thaleia was hoping this marriage would eventually bring the families closer than ever.

'Congratulations!' Agathi showered them with rice, tears of happiness in her eyes reflecting Thaleia's. She couldn't believe this day had come when she was marrying the love of her life who clearly felt the same way about her too.

These past weeks together had been blissful. Although she'd convinced him not to sell his yacht yet, worried he'd regret it, he was considering downsizing so the only crew needed was him and her. They'd both been busy with their businesses, but they always made time for one another, and he'd moved into her villa straight away so they could spend every night and morning together.

Enzo had proposed on this very beach two weeks ago, telling her that he wanted to be with her for ever. Something that was a huge step for him, and something he would never have promised if he didn't mean it. Thaleia already knew she wanted to spend the rest of her life with him so it had been an easy 'Yes'. She felt from the very depths of her soul that the two of them were meant to be together.

Enzo had whisked her to the altar as soon as possible, determined to show her she was the only woman for him when he'd spent his life running from commitment.

Together they'd been making plans to move into a bigger villa on Ithaca, with a view to starting a family. They'd talked it over a lot and decided that having children together was what they both wanted. Although they were going to travel the world first. Starting with their honeymoon in the Caribbean.

'I love you, Mrs Capelli,' Enzo said, staring at her with the utter devotion she knew he felt towards her because he showed it every day.

'I love you too, Mr Capelli.' She kissed him tenderly on the lips, enjoying the fact that she could do this any time she chose.

He was hers. She was his. And nothing else mattered.

* * * * *

Look out for the next story in the
A Pact Between Tycoons duet

Falling for the Grumpy Greek
by Suzanne Merchant

And if you enjoyed this story, check out these
other great reads from Karin Baine

A Nurse, a Pup, a Second Chance
The Tycoon's Festive Houseguest
Winter Nights with the Midwife

All available now!